LIMBUS

LIMBUS

JULIAN VAUGHAN HAMPTON

ACKNOWLEDGEMENTS

Praise and thanks to God for the liberty within my creativity. Thank to Becky, for your love and support. Thanks to Ann and Robert, for your guidance and foundation. Thanks to Tony, for your assistance. I also want to thank all of the friends and supporters not mentioned. Without you, this project and the ones that will follow would have been difficult to accomplish.
Thank you.
Anything is possible.
JVH

Limbus- *A Latin word meaning border or seam. The term Limbic System is derived from this word.*

"Limbus" by Julian Vaughan Hampton
ISBN 0-9771160-0-X

ISBN 13- 9780977116003
LLCN- 2005933541

This book is a work of fiction. Places, events, and situations in this story are purely fictional. Any resemblance to actual persons, living or dead, is coincidental.

Published by VAUGHANWORKS,
P.O. Box 18511
Milwaukee, Wisconsin, 53218,
www.vaughanworks.com
vaughanworks1@mfire.com
1-877-829-6757

Manufactured in the United States

Chapter 1

Pamela sat uncomfortably in her cubicle, sketching faces on the company stationary. Her mind roamed far from her job as a telemarketer. Instead, her thoughts rested on the art she loved; sculpting. Sculpting ran through her family's Sicilian bloodlines, from her grandmother, to her mother, down to Pam herself. The buzzer signaling the department's lunch break sounded, jolting her out of her daydream. Pam walked to the side of the last cubicle and waited for her friend Sylvia to join her.

"Hey girlfriend, are you ready to go?" Sylvia asked.

"Yeah, I guess," Pam sighed.

"What's wrong with you Pam?"

"I'll tell you when we get in the car," she replied.

The two women got into Sylvia's 1998 Chrysler Sebring. As they pulled off, Sylvia looked at Pam's somber face.

"Now tell me what's wrong, girl," Sylvia insisted.

"I'm so sick of this job, Sylvia. I want to quit and just focus on my sculpting, but Duncan would have a fit. He complains about the bills we have right now, and that's with both of our incomes. What should I do?"

Sylvia kept her eyes on the road while responding to Pam.

"You mean to tell me you're going to leave a thirty-five thousand dollar a year job to make heads out of clay? Good luck selling that idea to Duncan."

Tears slowly dripped from Pam's almond colored eyes.

"No, you don't understand," she cried. "I've wanted to make sculptures since I was a four year old playing with Play dough. Now I'm thirty-six years old and stuck in a job I hate. Creating images with clay and turning stone into life-like figures fills me with joy. Why shouldn't I have some joy in my life?"

Sylvia pulled her Chrysler into the parking lot of a fast food restaurant. She abruptly shifted the gear into the park position.

"What about your bills?" she asked. "Are you gonna make your husband pay all the bills?"

"Look, we've been living from paycheck to paycheck for the eight years we've been married. If I can sell a prized bust, I can make up to $50,000 doing something I love."

Sylvia looked stunned.

"You can make that much money sculpting?"

"Yeah, and sometimes you can make a lot more," Pam insisted.

Sylvia chuckled. "It'll be hard for Duncan to complain about fifty thousand dollars."

"Yeah, I know," Pam replied. "Plus, my old college professor told me I have a unique style many of the art dealers are looking for."

Sylvia pulled the keys out of the ignition. "You're serious about this, aren't you?"
Pam nodded, "I'm dead serious."
"Then go for it girl. I'm behind you one hundred percent."
They reached across the console to give each other a comforting hug. As they loosened their grip, they giggled at the sight of each other's tears.
"We are way too emotional," Sylvia said, smiling.
Pam wiped the tears from her eyes, and neatly ran her fingers through her autumn hair. She checked her makeup in the mirror within her visor and proceeded to eat lunch with Sylvia.

Pam returned to her department after lunch, and anxiously typed her letter of resignation. She struggled in her attempt to find the right words to use, staring at the blank page on the monitor for more than twenty minutes. Pam decided to use the standard form of resignation, leaving any personal feelings out of it. While removing it from the printer, she pondered whether or not to take it to her supervisor. Pam hoped he was somewhere else, so she could simply leave the letter on his desk. Out of the corner of his eye, Pam's boss made eye contact with her. She took a deep breath and walked hesitantly to his office. Pam knocked on the trim of his open door.
"Mr. Grady," Pam whispered.
Mr. Grady was on the telephone, and signaled to Pam to wait with his index finger.
"Yes sir, I'll do that. Thank you very much, and call me personally if you need anything else taken care of."

Hanging up the phone, he waived Pamela inside his office. After taking a deep breath, she entered the large room.

"Have a seat, Pam," said Mr. Grady.
She sat in the cloth chair directly across from Mr. Grady's plush leather chair. He removed his bifocals and leaned across the wood grained desk.

"Mr. Grady," Pam said quietly. "I have to resign from my position with the company."
Looking surprised, Mr. Grady responded.

"Is there something wrong with your position, or anything we can do to change your mind?"

"No sir, there's nothing wrong with the company, or with my position. Actually, it's a wonderful job."

"So what's with the letter of resignation?"
Pam replied, "Well sir, haven't you ever felt like there was something you were meant to do?"

"Yes Pam, I'd say so."

"Well, haven't you ever wished you'd taken the chance to do it?"

"Yes Pam, but do you really want to throw away such a promising opportunity for a dream?"

"Well, Mr. Grady, it's a chance I need to take," Pam replied sharply.

"I'll be honest with you. The company has big plans for you in the future. Are you sure you want to do this?"
"I'm sure, Mr. Grady."

"I have never been the one to stand in the way of an employee's progress. I see your mind is set on resigning."
Mr. Grady hunched his shoulders and signed Pam's request for resignation. Handing the paper back to Pam, Mr. Grady smiled.

"Good luck Pam. Give me a call if you charge your mind. Good employees like you are hard to find."
She extended her hand to Mr. Grady. "Thank you for understanding," said Pam, tightly squeezing his hand.

After work, Pam drove home, figuring she had a good three hours to decide how to break the news to her husband. As she pulled into the driveway, she parked behind Duncan's forest green pickup truck.
'What's he doing home,' she wondered. She walked through the screen door and found her husband sleeping on the couch with a six-pack of beer on the floor.
"Duncan, what's wrong? Why are you home?"
Duncan slowly turned his head toward Pam.
"They're making me work double shifts all this month. It's like they think I don't work hard enough as it is."
"Really," said Pam.
"Yeah, but at least we'll be able to finally pay off some of these old bills. The collectors keep leaving these damn messages."
Duncan arched his head back and quickly downed a can of beer. He sat the can on the old wooden end table and crushed it with the side of his balled palm.
"Honey," Pam said softly. "I need to talk to you about something."
"What's wrong now?"
"I resigned from my job today."
"You did what?"
"I resigned from my job today, so I can focus on my sculpting career."
Duncan began to sweat.

"How the hell do you think we're gonna pay these bills if you can't help me out?"

"Well, if I sell one of my sculptures, I could easily make five or ten thousand dollars."

"So what happens while you're waiting for someone to buy this stuff?"

Pam grew silent.

"Why didn't you tell me about this before you just went ahead and did it?"

Focusing on Duncan's beer, Pam responded.

"Because I knew you would act this way, especially if you were drinking."

Duncan became upset and kicked over the five beers remaining from his six-pack.

"So here we go about my drinking again. I work twelve to sixteen hours a day, while you want to play with clay and bitch about me having a beer after work. We got money for all this artistic bull crap, but I can't even put a new muffler on the truck or decent tires on the car."

Pam walked toward the kitchen, slamming every cabinet door she passed.

"That's why we don't have any money. You drank all our money away," she mumbled. "I should have never left Evansville." Pamela began tossing the empty beer cans into the trash.

Duncan looked at the tall grandfather clock, which read six o'clock.

"Damn, now I gotta go to work," Duncan said.

He spoke loud enough for Pam to hear every word. Grabbing his safety glasses, Duncan hustled out to his truck. Pam peeked through the blinds, watching her husband's truck rumble out of the driveway. A gray trail of smoke followed the truck's pathway.

After working three straight weeks of double shifts, Duncan had become disenchanted with his wife. He worked his thankless job each morning and night, while Pam worked on her sculptures. The bills piled up faster than Duncan's ability to pay them. Despite his occasional advances, Pam offered him little attention. He set his mind on being more spontaneous and romantic.

Duncan left work early to surprise his wife with a night out. He made reservations at Sir Lowell, an incredibly expensive French restaurant. While Pam worked on a sculpture in their bedroom, which looked as if it were converted into a studio, Duncan changed into his old military uniform. Pam loved to see Duncan in his uniform when he was on active duty. Some time had passed since then, and Duncan's was no longer the muscular soldier Pam once knew. With his large belly showing underneath his shirt, Duncan attempted to force the uniform to fit. He took a deep breath, and buttoned his uniform as much as he could, nearly tearing holes under his arms. He shaved his rugged beard and mustache and combed his wife's hair gel through his bushy hair, parting it on the left side. He sprinkled on the cologne Pam bought for him two Christmas's earlier. Duncan rumbled up the stairs, excited about his surprise. He peaked inside the bedroom door, knocking softly.

"Honey, I got a surprise for you," said Duncan. He held a bouquet of flowers hidden behind his back.

"I can't talk now. I need to finish this sculpture by tomorrow," Pam replied.

"Surprise," he screamed.

Bursting through the door, Duncan jumped through with the bouquet extended toward his wife. Startled, Pam cut the nose off her piece.

"Dammit Duncan! Why couldn't you just wait?"

She threw the scalpel to the floor.

"Now I have to start all over."

She smoothed the features off the face of the wet clay bust. Duncan left the bedroom and marched down the stairs.

"Duncan, I'm sorry," Pam called. "What did you want?"

Duncan pretended not to hear her. Pam was frustrated after her handsome sculpture began to look like a dead old man that had stared death in the face. The smeared features caused the sculpture's eyes to bulge and the mouth to freeze wide open. She continued to shake her head, doing all she could to repair the altered bust. Pamela smoothed the features off the face of the wet clay bust. Duncan tossed the flowers into the kitchen garbage, grabbed his work clothes and headed back to work.

He never made mention of his dinner plans. With all of the turbulence at his household, work didn't seem as bad as it previously had been. Working at the plant provided a convenient escape from the doldrums of his marriage. The couch became his personal bedroom and the alcohol became his solace.

There was an attractive engineer assigned to Duncan to help him complete a special project. She always seemed to give him the attention Pam couldn't afford to provide. Her name was Sierra Dimaano, and she held characteristics of both an Asian and European woman. She dressed business appropriate, save for her blouse which was consistently and intentionally open to the third button down. Sierra paid no mind to Duncan's oil stained uniforms, or his belly, which overlapped his belt. She gently stroked Duncan's ego until he was anxious to work his required double shifts.

"Duncan, I think we're finally finished," said Sierra, checking her calculator. "One hundred eighty-five degrees is the perfect temperature. I know I couldn't have done it without your expertise."

"Well, if you want to know about metals, I'm the man for the job," replied Duncan, roughly scratching his sweaty blonde scalp.

"I have to repay you for your help. Can I buy you a drink or something?" Sierra asked.

"Nah, that's alright. I'm just glad to be some help to somebody," said Duncan, sarcastically.

Sierra's eyes lit up. She had a fetish for underappreciated men, and Duncan was a prime candidate. She knew men would do anything for her if they were convinced she was the only one concerned about them.

"Now why would you think you're not a help to anyone? I'm sure a big, strong man like you is appreciated all the time."

"Nah, not me Sierra, but I'm alright," said Duncan. "I ain't worth feeling sorry for."
"Duncan, what's your last name?"
"It's Fontain," he replied.
"Duncan Fontain, damn that's a sexy name."
Duncan's pulse rose, causing his plastic safety glasses to become fogged. He removed them, and quickly wiped his brow. His green eyes focused on his young coworker. Sierra found the combination

of Duncan's Midwestern man and country boy personality to be very attractive.

"Well, at least let me buy you a drink after work."

"I don't think my wife would like that."

Sierra replied, "Don't worry. I'll have you back before six."

Duncan thought about it, and hit himself in the head with the palm of his hand.

"I forgot, I have to work doubles all this month. I won't have time to do anything but eat, sleep, and have a beer."

Sierra gave Duncan a wry smile. "Don't worry about it. I'll tell the company we need to check out some venders and price some new equipment. We do it all the time."

Duncan began to sweat. "Alright, just one drink," he said hesitantly.

"You have my word, teddy bear. Just one drink," said Sierra.

Weeks of hard work finally came to a standstill, as Pam put the finishing touches on her sculpture. The bust was an abstract image of John Quincy Adams. Aware of the city's plan to honor the man whom the city was named after, Pamela felt the need to create the bust. The gray sculpture began at the crown of the head and ended just below the shoulder. Many artists attempted to recreate the former president, but every work portrayed him as an angry man. Only Pam's sculpture was able to capture the gentle peacefulness within his rugged demeanor. The features were striking, down to the simulated wetness of the eyeball. Pam was pleased with her work.

She made a call to her former art professor. He had made a dramatic impression on Pam's life, and consistently urged his prized students to stay in touch with him. The call was answered on the first ring.

"Hello, this is Professor Wembly," he said in a withered voice.

"Mr. Wembly, this is Pamela."

"Pamela, how are you doing?" he asked, clearing his throat. "It's good to hear from you. I'd been meaning to contact you and a few of my other former students. A number of opportunities have opened up in the art world."

"That's what I called about, sir. I just finished a sculpture, and I feel it has a lot of promise."

"What type of sculpture, Pam?"

"Do you remember that Veneician style of sculpting you mentioned after your trip to Greece?"

"Yes, of course I do. Unfortunately, the one artist who perfected it passed away shortly after my return."

"Well, I paid close attention that day you taught us the style."

Mr. Wembly laughed. "You have one heck of a memory, Pam. I couldn't remember half of what I taught that day. Did you try that technique?"

"Actually, I created a new technique. I used the Venetian style and combined it with a style I picked up when we visited New Orleans."

"New Orleans? What kinds of artists work out of New Orleans?"

"The kind that don't make sculptures for the artistic merit, they make them to use in voodoo," Pam replied.

"That's nonsense. I hope you're not involved in any of that stuff, Pamela."

"No sir, I just used the style because it's so eerie. I even got a special type of clay to use. It's incredibly fragile, but it has a unique composition that gives the impression of human skin to a sculpture. It's a combination you need to see to believe."

"Well, I won't say I'm completely comfortable with that, but it sounds like an interesting concept," said Mr. Wembly. "In fact, there's a showing tomorrow for some major artist, and I'd like for you to consider attending."

"Do their pieces sell for a lot of money?" Pam asked.

"Pam, one man's junk is another man's art. The difference lies only in the perception of the buyer. Some dealers will pay between five and fifty-thousand dollars for each piece."

Pam sighed, "I could really use that kind of money."

"I've got an idea," shouted Mr. Wembly. "Pam, you are the best student I've ever taught. I'm going to put my neck out for you. How would you feel if I entered your work in an exclusive showing?"

Pam laughed. "My work could be in an exclusive showing? Are you serious? You could do that?"

"I'm the organizer of the event. Frankly, most of these so called artists aren't half as good as you. We need some new blood in the art world."

"What do I do, or what do you do? What comes next?" Pam asked.

"I'll enter your piece along with the other artists. At the end of the showing it will be up to the buyers and dealers to bid on it, or pass on it."

"Thank you so much, sir," said Pam.

"No problem, Pam. My job is to give my students the best opportunity for success. Meet me at the Galion Hall at six, and bring your sculpture."

"I will, sir. Thank you for your help."

"You're welcome," said Mr. Wembly before hanging up the telephone.

Around noon, Duncan and Sierra left work for a small bar hidden in the middle of the city.

"This is where I go to get away from everyone bothering me," she said.

"I need a place like that," Duncan replied.

"Well, you can share this place with me. You can get away anytime you want. I can keep a secret."

The bar was empty, except for Duncan, Sierra, and the bartender. The moody lights gave an impression of nightfall, though it was only twelve-thirty in the afternoon.

"I'll be right back," said Sierra as she sauntered to the restroom. Duncan paced around the bar. He peaked out the window to see if anyone knew he was inside. The bartender came beside Duncan.

"You seem a little anxious, buddy. Can I get you a drink?"

"How about a glass of Jack Daniels, straight?"

"Whatever you want," said the bartender. The bartender poured the liquor into a large glass. Duncan searched his pockets for his wallet.

"It's on my tab, Donnie," said Sierra in a sexy voice. Duncan turned around and noticed Sierra had changed her clothing. Her ankle length dress was hiked up and passed for a mini skirt, exposing her athletic legs. Her hair was let down, and hung to the small of her back.

"Damn," Duncan mumbled.

He grabbed his glass of Jack Daniels and downed it in one swallow. Duncan pounded his chest to relieve the burning from the alcohol. Sierra sat on the stool next to Duncan with her legs seductively crossed.

"What would you like to talk about, Mr.Fontain?"

"I don't know. Maybe work or something," said Duncan.

"Duncan, I didn't invite you out to talk about work. Why don't you tell me something about yourself? What makes you tick?"

Duncan smiled and thought about her questions.

"It's probably the same things that make any guy tick; work, beer, hunting, and football."

"Got any room for affection in that equation?" she asked.

"I don't know. That's up to ...my wife."

He stretched his neck to look outside the window.

"I gotta go."

"We just got here. Why don't you at least have another drink?"

"Nah, I think I should get home before..."

"Before what?"

"I just gotta go," said Duncan. "Thanks for the drink."

Duncan headed toward the door.

"Wait a minute," Sierra called.

"What is it?"

"I'll be making a few late night business runs, so call me if you want to schedule a personal meeting."

She handed Duncan a card with her number on the back. He grabbed the card and headed out through the door. While Duncan drove off, Sierra searched for her cell phone. She immediately called one of her friends.

"Hey Sheila, where's Ms. Long?" Sierra asked.

"You mean Tania? She's somewhere with a guy she met last Thursday. Don't change the subject. Is there anything you want to share?"

"What would you like to know," asked Sierra? She started giggling.

"Where were you at lunch time?"

"Let's just say this. By next week, I'll be ahead of you sixteen to fifteen."

"So you found one? What's he like?"

"He's a big guy, and he's kind of cute. His name's Duncan. He's like a giant teddy bear," said Sierra. "I'll give it a week, and he'll be doing anything I ask him to do."

"You know anything about his wife," Sheila asked.

"No, I didn't ask him about her yet. It seems like the same old situation. He's bustin his ass to pay the bills, and she won't appreciate him. Women like her make it easy for me to win the game. How many does Tania have?"

"After today, it will be seven."

"Aw, my little girl's growing up. How much did she get out of this one?"

"This one's just for numbers. She's lookin for blue collars after what happed with those doctors."

"That wasn't even my fault," said Sierra, laughing. "Nobody told him to take off his clothes in the middle of the park."

"You didn't have to call his girlfriend. She was checkin him in for about two hours. I think he got arrested for indecent exposure. I think he would have tried to kill you if he ever caught you."

"Girl, he shouldn't have been sweating me like that. Sometimes you gotta know when you're no longer wanted. That's what happens with those young guys. He thought he had it going on, but he was still wet behind the ears. At least I didn't do him like Tania did his friend. She had him chasing her car down the street with her underwear on."

Sheila began laughing.

"Don't you think we're getting a little too old to still play this game?"
There was a short pause in their conversation.
"Nah," they replied in unison.
"So how long do you think you're gonna keep this one," she asked.

"I kind of like him, so I'll probably keep him for a little while."

"Don't get serious on me, girl," said Sheila. "You know the rule; don't keep them longer than a month."

"I know the rule, Ms. Thurman. You don't even have to worry about that."

"Just call me if his wife interrupts our game."

"Girl, no one interrupts our game," said Sierra.

Chapter 2

Pam rushed through her best outfits to find something to wear to the exhibit. She found two sexy dresses that complimented her figure, but they weren't appropriate for the occasion. The black dress was Duncan's favorite, but the slit on the right side left little to the imagination. Pam removed it from its plastic covering, and after putting it on and taking it off more than five times, she placed it in the back of the closet. She settled on a quaint, light blue sundress with beige flowers, a tan straw hat, and a blue silk scarf wrapped around her neck. Pam had to dress quickly. The time was 4:08, and she needed to leave the house by 5:30.

While in the bathroom, Pamela heard the faint sound of her doorbell. She stretched her head toward the bathroom window, attempting to see through the glass and discover who was stationed at the front door. A tall silhouette stood outside her residence. Pam grabbed her bathrobe and walked toward the door. Tiptoeing to look though the glass, she saw Mr. Wembly. He looked incredibly distinguished in his black tuxedo, with his graying hair dyed jet black. Only his musky cologne provided evidence of his age. Pam cracked the door open.

"Mr. Wembly, what are you doing here?"

"I knew you'd have trouble finding the place, so I figured you could follow me there."

"That would be fine," said Pam. "Just have a seat and I'll be ready in a minute. Would you like something to drink?"

"What do you have?"

"I have water, milk, and beer. I haven't had time to go shopping lately."

"I'll have a beer, but just one. It'll be quite a trip," said Mr. Wembly.

She brought Mr. Wembly an unopened can of beer. He fumbled with the tab on the can.

"It's a little different than opening a bottle of wine, I guess."

"Here you go sir," said Pam, expertly pulling the tab open. "I have to finish getting ready. I'll be back in a little bit."

Mr. Wembly sat politely on the sofa, glancing at the pictures on the wall. He took a sip of his beer and his face turned sour.

'I don't know how men can drink this sewage,' he thought. He placed the nearly full can of beer on one of the table coasters. Pam went back upstairs to change her clothes, putting the final touches on her ensemble. She grabbed her sculpture and placed it in a large box. As she came down the stairs, Mr. Wembly hastily grabbed the nearly full can of beer. He pulled the can away from his lips.

"Ah, nothing like a cold one after a long day."

Pam smiled and walked away. Before the two left, she sprayed air freshener throughout the living room, attempting to eliminate Mr. Wembly's bad cologne.

Pam headed to the event with Mr. Wembly leading the way. The moody clouds were barely holding the rain from bearing down on their windshields. Pamela had never been to Galion Hall, but she had always heard rumors of its majestic setting. The site was more beautiful than her expectations. Extravagant cars lined the valet section in front of the building. Seven young men worked like clockwork, serving the high tipping patrons.

Mr. Wembly exited his forest green Jaguar and handed his keys over to an eager valet. Pam's blue 1993 cutlass supreme seemed completely out of place at the event. She stepped out of the vehicle and tentatively handed the keys over to the barefaced young man. Grabbing her ticket, she walked arm in arm with Mr. Wembly to the entrance. He shook another of the valet's hands, cleverly passing him a twenty dollar bill and whispering an order. The valet ran to Pam's car, quickly and carefully carrying her sculpture.

Pam gracefully glided through the pillar lined doorway, into the hall. Rows of elegantly diamond clad women stared at her, comparing her outfit to their own. Mr. Wembly stopped Pam near the rest of the artist.

"This is where we set up. Are you ready?" asked Mr. Wembly.

"I'm nervous, but yeah, I'm ready."

A black pedestal covered with an emerald green satin wrap was made available for each of the artists.

"Right here son," said Mr. Wembly to the valet. "Be very careful."

The valet grunted as he began lifting the box from the floor to the top of the pedestal. The soft lights enhanced the sculpture's features as much as the satin wrap. The artwork being shown was a collage of ideas from gifted people. There were abstract paintings, headless sculptures, and creations understood by only the creator. Groups of wealthy art connoisseurs freely roamed the display area.

Pam stood quietly confident as the prissy individuals circled the area. Their raised voices gave no indication which artwork the buyers found appealing, but most came to look at Pam's work numerous times. For more than an hour, buyers surveyed each piece. Moments later, a small group stopped near Pam.

"What a beautiful piece of work, my dear. Whom did you train under?" one lady asked.

"Doctor Wembly," Pam said enthusiastically.

"Walter Wembly? I knew that use of strand design on the hair looked familiar. How did you get those eyes to look so real?"

"I closed my eyes and imagined being face to face with him. I could feel him in my mind."

The lady looked confused. From behind them stepped an older man wearing a brown leather cowboy hat and a shirt lined with ruffles. Slowly, he inched forward with his stainless steel walker. He looked at Pam intensely with his gray eyes. The wrinkles around his face curled upward to form a smile.

"This is exactly what I hoped to find here," he said.

Pam walked toward the man, attempting to speak, but he quickly turned and shuffled away.

A smallish man dressed in a black tuxedo stepped up to the podium. He grabbed a crystal wand and struck it against the shimmering crystal bell sitting beside him.

"Here ye, here ye. We will now begin The Knights of Galion's 18th annual art exhibit and auction. I think everyone here knows the rules about bidding. If not, then you probably don't have enough money to participate."

The crowd let out a snobbish applause.

"Let's begin with our first piece. This oil painting is entitled 'Confusion'. The bidding will start at one thousand dollars."

Pam looked surprised.

"One thousand dollars," she whispered.

The bidding went around the room until there were no more signals given.

"Eight thousand going once, going twice, sold for eight thousand dollars."

The host turned to Pam's bust. Professor Wembly handed him a handwritten note. Quickly reading through the message, the host nodded at the professor. Word for word, he read from the letter.

"This next piece is a magnificent sculpture of John Quincy Adams. Its creator has done some of the most exquisite sculptures in the world. The bidding will start at five thousand dollars."

Pam grew concerned.

"No one would bid on a piece starting at five thousand dollars, would they?" she quietly asked.

Mr. Wembly patted her on the head.

"Don't worry, my dear. I told him to start the bidding that high."

An old, well-dressed man in the corner of the room raised his hand.

"I have a bid for five thousand dollars. Do I hear six thousand?"

A beautiful young woman near the front row raised her hand. Dressed in a skin tight red dress with diamonds caressing her neck, the woman looked at the man from the corner of her eye.

Six thousand, do I hear seven thousand?"

The old man with the cowboy hat raised his cane.

"Seven thousand, do I hear eight thousand?"

The young lady raised her hand again. She pulled out her shiny cherry dipped lipstick applied it to her full lips, blowing a kiss to the cowboy. Smacking his leather boots against his walker, the old man showed his frustration.

"Enough! If yawl keep this back and forth crap going on, I'm liable to die in my seat."

The crowd laughed.

"Dammit woman, stop playing with my money. One hundred thousand dollars," he screamed.

Pam's mouth dropped open. The room fell silent.

"Um...One hundred thousand going once, going twice, sold to the generous man with the brown cowboy hat for one hundred thousand dollars."

The young woman switched over to the old man, sitting in the chair next to him. She wrapped her arms around his wrinkled neck, removed his hat, and kissed him on top of his balding head.

"It's costing me too much money to keep you. If I knew it was gonna take this much, I would have stayed with my wife. Tell me why I need you again?" he asked.

The woman stood up, leaned over to blatantly expose her assets to him, and whispered something in his ear.

"Oh yeah, that's true. Gertrude can't do that, can she?" The couple laughed. His hands trembled, as he struggled to write a check.

"Hey you," he said, pointing to the announcer. "Send somebody over here to get this check. I gotta go. I don't wanna miss Matlock again."

Whispers filled the room, with individuals attempting to find out the identity of the wealthy man. The consensus was the old man was a relative of John Quincy Adams himself. He raised the check in his shaking hand, until one of the ushers took it from him. Pamela could hardly breathe due to the excitement. She turned to Mr. Wembly.

"Is this for real?"

"Of course it's real, Pam. We don't dabble in monopoly money here, my dear."

"So when do I get the money?"
"You can have it as soon as you want it."

"Can I get it now? I really need it."

Sure you can, Pam," said Mr. Wembly. "The check goes to the treasurer in the back, who takes off ten percent for commission. After the commission's taken, he'll write a check from the Knights of Galion I your name."

"Is that all there is?"

"Yes, my dear. That's all there is, except for a nice thank you for me."

Pam leaned over and gave Mr. Wembly a friendly kiss on the cheek. She exited through the curtains to the treasurer's office at the rear of the building. There sat an elderly woman next to a large man donning a black security guard uniform. He stood protectively over her with his hand fixed to the trigger of his glock.

"Excuse me ma'am," Pam whispered.

The guard gave Pam an ill glare.

"No one is allowed back here until the show is finished," said the guard.

"Oh, I'm sorry. I didn't know."

Mr. Wembly peeked through the curtains.

"Reggie and Margaret, she's with me."

The guard's angry face settled and his fingers lapsed from the trigger.

"Well, come here honey. I didn't know you were here with Mr. Wembly," said the old lady.

Pam crept over toward the table. Margaret signed the check as the guard signed the booklet witnessing the transaction. She handed the check over to Pam, who looked stunned at the amount. The check was worth ninety thousand dollars.

"Sorry dear, we have to take off ten percent of every piece to raise money for the hall."

"This is mine? This is all for me?"

"Yes dear, it's all yours. Have a nice day."

"Thank you very much," said Pam. She sprinted happily toward the exit.

With debating thoughts of Sierra still in his head, Duncan entered his home. He immediately came upon the foul odor of discount cologne being blanketed by air freshener. The combination of scents made him nauseous, as much as the sight of Pam's lace underwear scattered across the bedroom floor.

"I knew it," he screamed.

He angrily kicked over the lamp on the nightstand and sulked downstairs to grab a beer from the refrigerator. When Duncan reached the living room, he noticed a full beer on the loveseat.

'No one sat on the love seat except Pam, and she don't drink,' he thought.

Stagnant in his recliner, he waited impatiently for Pam to arrive. Uncanny ideas of what 'some man' was allowed to do with his wife haunted Duncan. He rose up to look around their bedroom once more. There were Pam's unmentionables, a few discarded provocative outfits, and a plastic cover. It was the plastic cover, which protected Pam's favorite form fitting black dress. Duncan had been dying to get Pam to wear it for years. He threw the cover on the unmade bed.

Duncan headed back to the refrigerator, this time grabbing two bottles of beer. He plopped down in his chair, slumping deeper in the cushion with every swallow of alcohol. He focused on the cherry wood grandfather clock with the copper hands. Every second he watched the moving hands brought additional anger to Duncan's state.

Concern led to frustration, as thoughts of revenge began to creep into his mind.

"I should have known she was screwin around with somebody," Duncan mumbled over and over.

All rational thoughts concerning the possibility of Pam's faithfulness were whisked away by the time he drank his sixth beer. He searched his trouser pockets for Sierra's perfume scented business card, but was unable to find it. He also checked his coat pockets, but had no success. Duncan finally thought to look in his pickup truck. Staggering his way to the vehicle, he found Sierra's card on the driver's side runner.

Walking back inside the house, he grabbed the vanilla colored cordless phone off its base, and began dialing the number. After numerous mistake filled attempts to dial Sierra's phone number, he finally pressed the correct numbers. The phone rang two or three times before she answered.

"Sierra Dimaano, talk to me," she said rigidly.

"Sierra, this is...a...Duncan. You know, Duncan from...a...work."

"Hey Duncan, I didn't think you were gonna call."

"Yeah, I wasn't gonna call, but somethin changed my mind. What were you up to tonight?"

"I was just taking care of business. I just finished meeting with a client, so I'm going home to pour myself a drink and take a hot bubble bath."

"I hear that," said Duncan. "That's what I'm doing."

"You're in the tub?'

"Nah, I'm just pouring myself a drink. In fact, I've been pouring myself drinks all night."

"Oh yeah, did you save any for me?"

"I keep drinks around me at all times. When everything in your life is as screwed up as mine, it helps you forget the pain."

Duncan looked at his half empty bottle and poured the beer down his throat.

"So are you gonna share," prodded Sierra.

"Share with you? What are you saying?"

"Are you calling to invite me over, or what?"

"You might as well come over," Duncan muttered. "I could use the company."

As Duncan placed the phone on the receiver, stacks of envelopes fell to the floor and were trampled under his aimless prowl. Nearly slipping on the papers, Duncan became annoyed by the enveloped containing the bills. He ripped open the bills addressed to Pam, staring at every item she purchased during the month. It was the first time in their marriage he ever opened her mail. There were enormous amounts of arts and craft supplies charged to Pam's credit cards. Duncan threw them all on the coffee table.

Duncan didn't think Sierra would actually come over, until the doorbell disturbed his drunken catnap. He clumsily rambled to the door, expecting to see his untimely wife's attempt to enter through the chained front door. Duncan unlocked the door, swinging it wide open. Outside the entrance stood Sierra, dressed in a navy blue business suit with a white dress shirt opened to the fourth button. A large black Englishman's umbrella covered her slightly wet hair from the strengthening drizzle.

"We'll aren't you gonna let me in?" Duncan walked back into the living room, leaving the door wide open for Sierra to enter.

"I thought you'd be a little happier to see me," said Sierra.
She let down her umbrella and sat on the large sofa, while Duncan hopped back into his favorite chair. He stared blankly at the dark television screen with one hand on the remote control and the other holding his nearly empty beer bottle.

"So what are we watching?" asked Sierra, sarcastically. "Aren't you going to get me a drink?"

"Oh, I'm sorry. You want a beer or something?"

"Yes, if you don't mind."
Duncan moved sluggishly toward the kitchen to get Sierra a beer.

"That's ok, I have one," said Sierra, playfully.

Duncan turned to find Sierra sitting in his recliner with his beer in her hand.

"Give me that," Duncan groaned.

He slowly reached for the bottle, but she pulled it away.

"Come and get it."

Duncan sat back on the sofa.

"That's alright, you can have it. There ain't that much left anyway.

Sierra drank the remainder of Duncan's beer. Sitting on the end of the loveseat, Duncan finally turned on the television. Sierra jumped on his lap and began running her fingers through his hair. Fighting to keep his wits about him, Duncan began to nod off. Sierra kissed him on his forehead.

"Alright, I'm going to bed," said Duncan. "You can let yourself out, but you better leave soon. My wife's probably on her way home."

He crawled up the stairs and fell sound asleep the instant his head hit the pillow. Sierra tiptoed after him and lay next to him. Her attempts to get his attention failed, from kisses on his neck to the thrusts to his ribs. She snuggled next to him for an hour before giving him a goodbye kiss on the cheek. Duncan responded to her kiss with an even louder snore.

"Goodnight sleepyhead," she responded.

Sierra hustled down the stairs, grabbed her coat and left the house. The rain had become a downpour, so she pulled off her high heels and quickly raced to her SUV. She wiped the rain from her forehead and pinned her hair into a bun. By the time she left the block, Sierra realized she had forgotten her umbrella.

'I hope he picks up the phone before Miss Thang gets home,' she mumbled.
She called frantically, hanging up each time Pam's voice reached the answering machine.
    "Oh well. I ain't gonna cry over spilled milk."
She cruised away, steering the car with her left pinkie and applying lipstick with her other hand. When she was more than two miles away, Sierra changed her mind.
    'Ain't no way I'm gonna let go of a two hundred dollar umbrella for a boring ass night,' she thought.
Sierra turned her truck around and drove back to Duncan's house.

    Pam raced home, anxious to tell Duncan about their financial gain. The rain began to fall slightly faster, causing her to set the wipers to their highest position. Pam was lost, but used the taillights of the vehicle ahead of her to find her way to a familiar road. The trip home took much more time than the route Mr. Wembly used to get to the hall. Her relief came when she saw her husband's forest green truck in their driveway. Excited, she missed her driveway and parked her car in front of her neighbor's house. She rushed toward the frond door. When she pushed her key into the keyhole, the unlocked door swung wide open and crashed into the wall.
    "Duncan, guess what happened," she screamed.
There was no response.
    "Duncan?"
    She walked through their house, looking for her husband. He wasn't in his favorite chair, but

the trail of beer bottles led to the bathroom. The light was visible under the bathroom door, and Pam could hear the water running.

"Duncan, guess what," she called, knocking on the door.

She ripped open the envelope containing the check and a letter, dropping the envelope on the floor. Again, there was no response. She slowly turned the knob and peaked into the bathroom.

"Duncan," she screamed.

The faucet was running, but the bathroom was empty. She turned off the cold water and headed back to the living room. Her eyes caught hold of a long black umbrella leaning against the trim near the front door.

'Whose umbrella is this,' she thought.

Pam couldn't recall anyone she knew who may have owned the umbrella. She snatched it up and ran up the stairs. Drops of water trickled down her wrist and on to the carpet.

"Duncan," she shouted.

She could hear his snoring halfway up the stairs. The bedroom door was wide open. Duncan lay flat on his back in the center of the bed. His left hand was tucked in the front of his jeans, with his right hand holding his last beer.

"Duncan," she called.

Duncan turned his head, exposing the two red lip prints pasted on the side of his face. Pam could feel her heart beating. She smacked him in the stomach with the umbrella.

"What the hell," Duncan screamed.

"Who was here, Duncan?"

"What are you talking about?"

Pam thrust the umbrella inches away from Duncan's nose.

"One of my friends came over for a minute."

Pam began to cry. She threw the nearly dry umbrella at his head.

"I guess your buddy wears lipstick, huh dumb ass?"

Duncan leisurely raised his hand to his face. He wiped the right side of his face and found nothing. When he wiped the left side, his palm turned red from the lipstick. He took a deep swallow.

"Its not what it looks like."

Pam struggled to complete her sentences.

"Why ...how could you do this?"

Duncan became defensive.

"How could I? How could you? You come in here at the middle of the night. Where were you all night?"

"Don't change the subject," Pam screamed. "You let some woman come into our home. You have lipstick on your face. You want to complain about where I've been?"

"Look at what time it is," said Duncan pointing to the clock. "Where were you?"

"I was making money," she answered.

She pulled out the check from the auction and held it inches away from his face.

"I was with my art professor."

"So that's how you make your money now," Duncan blurted out.

He immediately grabbed her shoulders.

"I didn't mean that."

"Let me go," she cried. "How could you say that about me?"

Tears poured down Pam's face. She slowly backed away from him. Duncan moved forward to embrace her.

"I can't believe you said that."

Pam's hand trembled as she covered her mouth. The tears walked across her fingers and she found it hard to breathe. She turned and ran down the stairs. At the same time, Sierra was pulling into the driveway.

'Well, the wife's not home yet,' she mumbled. 'I need my umbrella.'
She knocked softly on the door.

"Duncan, open the door," she whispered.
'I'll give him ten seconds, and then it's his fault if she finds my umbrella.'
Sierra began tapping her foot, as she counted down.

"Ten, nine, eight..."
Pam heard the whisper.

"Seven, six, five..."
She moved toward the door.

Four, three, two..."
She looked through the window and saw Sierra.

"One..."
Pam flung the door wide open. Sierra was knocked two steps back, nearly falling down the front stairs. Pam's anger momentarily held her tears.

"Who the hell are you?" she asked
Sierra continued to stumble, walking backward toward her vehicle.

"I just work with him, that's all," said Sierra.

"Did you sleep with my husband?"

"No, I promise...nothing happened."
Hearing the commotion, Duncan made his way downstairs.

"Pam, what are you..." Sierra?"

"Is that your whore's name?"

"I barely know her. You should know me well enough to know I wouldn't want someone like that," said Duncan, motioning up and down Sierra's outfit.

Pam reached for Sierra's face, digging her nails into her forehead. Sierra slapped Pam's hand away and ran to her vehicle. She held her bleeding face in both hands. Sierra sped away from the house. Pam threw a large stone at her rear window, shattering the glass. Afterwards, Pam's attention turned back to Duncan. She looked into his eyes.

"How could you," she sighed, pounding on his chest.

"Nothing happened, Pam."

She began to cry, grabbing her keys and running to her car. Pam struggled to catch her breath as she jumped into the car. She angrily slammed the door. Reaching into her glove compartment, Pam frantically searched for her asthma inhaler. The windows became fogged immediately. Finally grabbing the inhaler, she took a deep breath. Outside the vehicle stood Duncan, soaked and pounding on the glass. Pam sat in the car more than twenty minutes with her hands on her keys set in the ignition.

Chapter 3

Sierra drove to her friends' house, continuously checking the deep scratches in her face through the rear view mirror. Drops of blood dribbled from her forehead and down the bridge of her nose. She pounded the steering wheel with her left hand. Arriving at Sheila's house, Sierra marched up the porch and rapidly rang the doorbell. The door swung open.

"Damn, what is it?" asked Sheila.

"Look at this. Look at what she did to my face."

"Who did that to you?"

"Duncan's wife did it."

"Did she catch you two together?"

"No, she didn't catch us. We didn't do anything. I went over to his house, just to visit. He tried to get with me, but I wasn't about to give him some. I was just teasing him. I wanted to see how hard he would sweat me. I forgot my umbrella, and when I went back for it, she was there."

"Girl, couldn't this wait until the morning? I'm trying to get some rest, and here you come ringing my doorbell."

"You need to stop trippin. This is still my house, whether I let you rent it or not. You're just lucky I'm not here to collect rent."

"I'm just kidding, Sierra," said Sheila, nervously.

"I just can't believe you let her do that to your face."

"I didn't let her do it to me. She scratched me before I could do anything. You know I wouldn't let anybody do that to me. Remember what happened to the other girl that messed with me?"

"Yeah, she still ain't got her teeth fixed," answered Sheila.

Tania came down the stairs.

"Damn girl, who whooped your ass?"

Sheila interrupted Sierra's response.

"The wife of her big teddy bear," she said with a smirk.

Sheila turned to Sierra.

"So what are you gonna do?"

"I don't know," Sierra replied.

"She messed up your face. Why don't we go mess up her face?"

Sierra looked enthused.

"So what can we do to her?"

"Girl, I don't know. Let's go over there, and whatever happens, just happens.

The three women drove to Pam's house in Sheila's red Dodge Durango with tinted windows. They saw Pam's car in front of her neighbor's home, while Duncan stood frustrated outside her car. When Sheila observed the exhaust billowing from Pam's tailpipes, she began to patiently trail the vehicle.

Pam heavily pressed her foot on the accelerator. Duncan continued to yell, being drowned out by the revving engine. The tires squealed as she raced away from her husband, with the red Durango not far behind. The wipers flattered full speed, while the rainfall grew more intense. Pam could barely see the road past a few feet. She removed her clouded glasses, tossing them to the floor of the passenger's side. Pamela coughed and gasped, attempting to stem her crying. The further she drove; the more darkness she encountered. Inside the truck, Sheila and Sierra argued.

"Girl, why are you drivin so slow?" asked Sierra. "She's gonna get away."
"I got this, OK? I'm waiting for the right moment."
"I don't give a damn about the right moment. Just run her off the road."
"In a minute," said Sheila. "I got this."
As Pam continued to drive, the street lights grew further apart. Soon after, there were none in sight. There were no cars in the vicinity, except for the lone vehicle trailing Pam. Panic began to set in, intensifying with every passing moment. Angry and frightened, she looked to the sports utility vehicle behind her for assistance. Pam put on her turn signal and moved into the right lane of the lane road. The Durango followed her into the right lane. Rolling down her widow, Pam reached through the driving rain to urge the Durango to pass.

"Do it now," screamed Sierra.
"I got this, girl," said Sheila.
Tania came from the back seat and leaned over Sierra's shoulders. Sheila crept closer to Pam's car. Sierra became impatient.

"Damn girl, just do it," she said. Sierra stretched her leg over to the driver's side of the vehicle and stomped on the accelerator. The Durango jolted forward, slamming into the rear of Pam's car. Pam's head snapped back violently as her hands left the steering wheel. She shrieked and jammed the brake pedal. The tires failed to provide any traction, as the car left the road. The car flew through the air and crashed into a ditch along the side of the road. Pam's head banged against the steering wheel. She lay, slumped against the door, bleeding from her nose and mouth. The car was pointed upward from within the ditch. The women in the Durango pulled up slowly to check out the accident.

"Do you think she's dead?" asked Sheila. She lowered the window to see inside Pam's car.

"I don't know, but we better get out of here.

Pam looked up at the vehicle.

"Help me, please," whispered Pam. Her blood stained hand streaked down the glass.

"I think she saw you," said Sheila. Sierra punched the accelerator, crashing into Pam's car once more. The car was knocked deeper into the ditch. Pam screamed before passing out. The vehicle quickly drove away.

The mangled shell of the car twisted around Pamela's body. As the night moved on, Pam faded in and out of consciousness. A deer hunter traveling from the north passed the scene of the accident. The car's one remaining headlight was still on, but grew dim due to the draining of the car battery. He pulled his pickup truck over and walked down the slope on the side of the road. The hunter peered through the space that was formerly the driver's side window and saw Pam, bloodied and bruised. He tried to open the door, but the damage was extensive. Running to the rear of his truck, he grabbed a tire iron to pry the door open, but merely bent the body.

Entering his vehicle, the man drove to a small cabin along the back road. Knocking on the door, he screamed, "Help, somebody, I need help!"

The cabin door opened and the deer hunter bolted through.

"I need to use your phone."

"Hold on, boy," said the gray haired man. "What's the problem?"

Breathing heavily, the hunter responded. "Some lady crashed on Saso's curve. I don't even know if she's alive."

"Oh my goodness," replied the old man. "Well boy, you can use the old phone over there. She's old, but she'll still work for you."

The hunter stuck his head in the small wooden booth. There was an old dusty phone with a rotary dial on next to it. He called 911 for help, before returning to the wreck.

By the time the ambulance arrived, Pam was unconscious. The medical team called for additional support. Only the use of the Jaws of Life enabled them to extract her from the crumpled vehicle. Her heart rate and breathing were normal, but she was suffering a tremendous amount of blood loss from her head. The medics continued to slow the bleeding while Pamela was being transported to the hospital.

She arrived at the hospital nearly forty-five minutes later. Rushing her through the quiet hallways, the doctor's worked frantically on her face. The impact of the steering wheel had caused her eyes to blacken and swell from the bleeding. The medical assistants searched Pam's belongings and found her husband's information. The youthful assistant called to inform Duncan of the situation.

Duncan was sitting in his chair with his hands supporting his head. The telephone rang, and he slowly answered.

"Yeah, who is it?"

"May I please speak to Duncan Fontain?

"This is Duncan," he answered.

"Mr. Fontain, this is the Quincy Wellness Center. Your wife Pamela has been involved in an accident. I think it would be in your best interest to see her ASAP. Do you know where we are located?"

"Yeah, I pass your place when I go up north. Is she alright?"

"Sir, she's in surgery right now. As soon as you arrive, the doctors will be able to share some more of the details with you."

Duncan took a deep breath and responded.

"All right, I'll be there in a minute."

As the doctor's performed the surgery to relieve the pressure of the blood in Pam's face, she lost consciousness and slipped into a coma. Duncan arrived at the hospital, parking his truck in a reserved handicap parking space and running toward the door. He stopped at the service desk.

"I'm looking for Pamela Fontain's room. She just got into surgery."

"Oh, let me see," said the receptionist. "She's in room 403."

Duncan looked around the area. The receptionist pointed to the right.

"That's through the elevator on the right, get off on the fourth floor, and it's the first door on the left."

"Thanks," responded Duncan.
He rumbled to the elevator, breathing heavily as the numbers changed. When the doors opened,

there was a great deal of commotion around the first room to the left.

"Sir, you can't come in here," said one of the nurses.

"Ain't this Pamela Fontain's room?"

"Yes it is. Are you her husband?"

"Yeah, I'm her husband," Duncan responded.

"I'll get a doctor to explain what's going on."

The nurse informed the doctor of Duncan's arrival. The doctor approached him. Removing the gloves, he shook Duncan's hand.

"Hello Mr. Fontain, I'm Doctor Hammonds. I'm glad you came so soon. We're having a little trouble taking care of your wife."

"What kind of trouble?" asked Duncan.

"She's not responding to any stimulus we use. We're also having a bit of trouble with the significant amount of blood loss."

"Is she alright?"

The doctor moved in closer to Duncan.

"We don't think she's in any imminent danger, but we're monitoring her cerebral condition. She suffered a pretty severe injury to her head."

"Can I talk to her?"

"Give us another hour or so to get everything under control, and we'll be able to let you see her. You must remember; she won't be able to respond to you."

"I understand, doctor."

Duncan sat in the waiting area, staring at the pictures lining the walls. His foot tapped constantly, irritating the one other visitor sitting across from him. The middle-aged woman sighed in an obvious attempt to interrupt Duncan's noise.

The doctors worked furiously, finally stabilizing Pam's condition, but she remained in a coma. She was hooked up to an intracranial pressure monitor to further analyze her injuries. After all the tests were performed, the surgeon came out to provide Duncan with the information.

"Hello Mr. Fontain. I'm Doctor Bradley."

"How's Pam?"

"Unfortunately she's still in a coma." Duncan scratched his head.

"When a subject is in a coma, it's a deep state of unconsciousness where her psychological and motor responses to stimulus are impaired, and seem to be lost."

"What the hell does that mean?" Duncan asked.
"Your wife is alive, but she's not simply sleep. That's probably the most simplistic way I can phrase it. Does that help you understand a little better?"

"Yeah, I guess. So what are you gonna do next?"

"We've positioned her to keep her airways cleared. We'll also perform a neurological assessment every four hours."

"Then what are you gonna do next?"

"Once we determine the full extent of her injury, we'll start the most difficult part of the surgery. Right now, we have her on a psycho stimulant medication called Permax."

Two police officers stepped in between their discussion. The smaller officer stood behind Duncan with his hand wedged in his belt. The large officer place his hand on Duncan's back.

"Excuse me doctor. We need to have a word with this guy."

"That's fine officer. I have more work to do," said the doctor.

"Are you Mr. Fontain?" asked the larger officer.

"Yeah that's me," Duncan replied.

The smaller officer stepped in.

"You got some identification?"

"No, I don't have my identification. I came here as fast as I could."

"You got to have something that identifies you."

"Look officer, I just want to go in and see my wife."

The smaller officer began to sweat.

"We'll what's your wife's name?"

"It's Pam Fontain, I mean...Pamela Fontain."

The larger officer put his hand on the chest of his partner.

"My name is Lieutenant Douglas. I'm the investigative lieutenant for Quincy. This is Officer Davis. We're gonna let you go, but we'll be in touch with you to get some more information. We'd like to advise you not to leave the town."

"Look officer, I don't know what happened to my wife," said Duncan.

"He said we'll get back in touch with you," said Officer Davis. "Nobody asked you to talk back."

Duncan's face turned red. He stared into the eyes of the annoying officer. Mumbling under his breath, he turned and walked into Pam's room.

"You're lucky you got a badge on," he whispered.

"I heard that," said Davis. "You better watch yourself."

Duncan walked away, steaming. He held his tongue once again. Since he was very young, he had always tried to hold his temper. Duncan was much larger than the other children in his neighborhood. Most of them were afraid of him due to his size, so he worked hard to show his kind nature. His gentle disposition became so much a part of him, he avoided altercations all together. Duncan's childhood desire to become a professional football player soon faded. His strength, size, and aggressiveness that were attributes necessary to become a great football player were sacrificed just to fit in. Although he did finally become "just one of the guys", Duncan also became a pushover. He thought his military service would have changed his approach to challenges, but serving his country had no effect on his personality. The bullying of the officers was just another incident in which he failed to fight back.

Duncan entered Pam's room and noticed a security guard sitting on the side of the door. The nurse was next to Pam, adjusting her pillow. Walking over to Pam, Duncan patted her on the hand.

"Sir, I'll have to ask you not to touch the patient," said the guard.

Duncan retreated to the chair closest to Pamela's bed. Ten hours a day, he sat next to Pam. He spoke softly about the memories they shared from the time they first met, up to their sixteenth wedding anniversary.

"Remember our first date, honey? I was nervous about everything. I wanted to make the best impression on you, so I sold my Bear's tickets to buy you that necklace and those flowers. I guess I started things off wrong. You probably thought I had a lot of money then, hun? You were so beautiful. I would have sold my season tickets for you. Well, maybe not those games against the Packers. Remember when I tried to take you to that French Restaurant, and order the food for us? I thought that I was ordering duck, but they gave us squid because of my bad French. You were a good sport. You didn't complain or badmouth me or nothing. You just said, 'It's really good'. I knew you hated it, because I could hardly keep my food down. It was just nice to be there with you. I don't know how a fat slob like me could ever get a woman like you, but somehow it happened. I guess every dog has its day."

When Duncan wasn't at the hospital, he was at work. He ate at work, showered at work, and slept during his lunch hours. Sierra was assigned to a project with another company, so Duncan's work days were fairly mundane. It wasn't until Duncan was approached by one of his coworkers that things became more interesting.

"Man, I'm glad it's Friday," said the coworker. "I can't wait to get outta this hell hole."

"Yeah, I hear you Donald. It's been a rough couple of weeks."

"I know it's been rough for you. Is Pam doing any better?" asked Donald.

Duncan sighed, "Not really. I don't even think she knows I'm there most of the time."

Donald patted Duncan on the back.

"So what are you gonna do if things don't work out?"

"What do you mean?"

Donald hesitantly continued.

"You know what I mean. What if she don't wake up? What if she's like a zombie or something?"

"Damn Donald. Way to pick my spirits up."

Duncan began to walk away, as Donald followed him.

"Hold on, Duncan. I'm just saying; you never know what is going to happen to her, so you gotta make sure everything's taken care of."

"I think we'll be alright," said Duncan. "As long as I work here, and with the money Pam made, I'll be alright."

"How much money does Pam have?" Donald asked.

"She made about ninety-thousand selling some art work."

"Damn, ninety-thousand?"

"Yeah, about that," said Duncan.

Donald wiped his forehead.

"Whew, that's a lot of money. Does she have a will?"

"She ain't dead, man. She's in a coma."

"What condition is she in?"

"The doctor said she's in critical condition."

"I suggest you get her to sign a will as soon as she can," said Donald. "I know this guy who's wife had a ton of money stashed away. When she died, the government got all of it. He had to borrow money just to bury her. Guess why he didn't get any money?"

"She didn't write it in a will?"

Donald nodded adamantly.

"She didn't write it in a will."

"I gotta get back to work, Don. Thanks for the advice."

"Any time, man," replied Donald.

Pamela's comatose condition lasted four weeks, until there was a dramatic change. One of the nurses was in the process of changing her bandage and prepping her for the night. The nurse often talked to Pam while checking on her condition.

"Wow, those wounds are healing pretty well."

She cleaned and wrapped Pam's head in a new dressing. Pam's hand moved toward the nurse. The nurse jumped back, startled by the sudden motion. She ran to the intercom.

"I need a doctor in room 12B."

Slowly opening her eyes, Pam turned toward the doctor's entering the room.

"Where am I? Who...what...is...," she mumbled.

"I need you to lay back Mrs. Fontain," said Doctor Bradley.

"My head hurts real bad," Pam screamed.

The nurse came around the doctor.

"You've been in a serious accident and injured your head."

The doctor gave Pam some painkillers.

"This should ease the pain a little."

"Why can't I feel my hand," said Pam, pointing toward her right hand.

"Don't worry, Mrs. Fontain. Sometimes it takes a little time to regain all of your muscular capabilities. It's just a side effect of a coma."

"A coma...I've been in a coma? How long have I been...in a coma?"

"About four weeks, Pam."

Duncan walked into the room, surprised to see his wife sitting upright and awake, yet groggy.

"Honey, you're out of it," shouted Duncan.

He ran toward Pam, only to be interrupted by the doctors.

"Be gentle sir. She still has a lot of recovering to do."

"Oh, I'm sorry doctor."

Duncan crouched beside Pam's bed, kissing her on the side of her face.

"I thought I was going to lose you."

"Duncan, I can't feel my hand," said Pam, crying.

"It's alright honey. We'll get through this."

He sat next to her, softly rubbing his palm across the back of her hand. Four hours later, the head surgeon walked in.

"I hate to disturb the both of you, but we've found some serious results in your tests. Under normal circumstances, I wouldn't speak to a patient about surgery. This happens to be anything but normal."

The doctor put the x-ray up to the screen.

"As you can see here, there are damaged blood vessels higher up the brain stem and within the limbic system. There's a lot of swelling within the tissue near that region. If we don't repair the area, along with the temporal lobes, there could be a complete loss of cognitive skills, including your language skills. It is imperative we perform surgery on that area immediately."

Duncan jumped up.

"Come on, doctor. She just got out of a coma, and you want to do surgery."

"I understand your concern, but I wouldn't have mentioned this if it wasn't of a dire nature."

"How often do you guys do this type of stuff?"

"Brain injuries are common place in my field. There's never an easy one, but your wife's is significantly more complicated than the other's I've done. As serious as the surgery is, the results of performing it are even more distressing."

"I'll be alright when it's over, right doctor?" Pam asked.

The doctor moved away from the screen.

"I'll be honest with you, Pam. Even with the surgery, we're looking at a twenty to thirty percent chance of success. The more we wait, the more that percentage drops. We do have one of the best neurosurgeons in the nation at the Quincy Wellness Center."

Walking over to the desk, the doctor grabbed a clipboard full of papers.

"I'll give you a little time to discuss the procedure and look over the papers.

"These are liability waivers, authorizations for surgery, and other forms we need filled out to get started. There's really not much of a choice, folks."

The doctor gave a forced smile, and slowly closed the door.

"Not much of a choice. Wow."

"I guess we have to do this?"

"Yeah, I guess so."

Duncan began to think about what Donald said. He hesitantly pulled a piece of paper out of his pocket. It was crumbled and written in a permanent marker. It read, 'I do hereby leave all of my possessions and the assets thereof to Duncan Fontain'. On the top, large letters read WILL.

"I think this is something you should look at," said Duncan.

The nurse walked in while Duncan was passing the paper to Pamela.

"A will...You wrote a will for me? What...Are you expecting me to die?"

"No, it's not that. It's just that the government..."

"Damn the government," said Pam. "You're supposed to support me."

Tears welled in Pam's eyes.

"I don't even care anymore. I'll just sign it. I'll sign everything."

Pam began to psychotically sign all the forms, including the will. She awkwardly used her left hand.

"Here, take them!"

She threw all the papers to Duncan, who merely held his head down.

"Mrs. Fontain, you'll have to calm down," said the nurse.

"Could you tell the doctor I'm ready for the surgery, nurse," Pam asked.

"Yes ma'am," she replied.

"Pam, I'm sorry...we had to talk about..."

"We didn't have to do this, Duncan. It didn't have to happen this way. First you cheat on me, and then you want me to sign a will. You're probably waiting for me to die."

"No, that's not it. My friend Donald told me about someone he knew who didn't have a will, and lost everything."

"I don't care about Donald," said Pam "What about me? Don't you think I've gone through enough?"

Pam began to cry even more.

"Just leave. I don't need this stress right now. If I don't make it through this, you can take all the money and go with that broad you were with."

"But Pam, I..."

"Get out of here, Duncan!"

Duncan walked out of the room, sitting in the corner of the visitor's waiting room. There was a knock on Pam's hospital door.

"One moment, please," said Pam, wiping her face. "Alright, you can come in."

The doctor entered the room.

"So, are we going to go ahead with the procedure?"

"Yes doctor, I'm ready."

"Where's your husband? Is he OK with this?"

"Oh yeah, he's more than OK with the surgery."

"So when would you like to begin," asked the doctor?

Pamela took a deep breath.

"Right now," she answered.

"Are you sure?"

"We can do it right now," said Pam.

"Well, let me take these papers up front and we'll begin the process."

The surgeon walked from Pam's room and noticed Duncan rambling back and forth in the visitor's lounge.

"Mr. Fontain, we'll be putting Mrs. Fontain under very shortly, so now would be the time to see her. If there is anything important you wish to say, I wouldn't hold back. This will be a touchy procedure."

He patted Duncan softly on the shoulder and walked toward the service desk. Moving timidly toward the room, Duncan peeked in the open door.

"Pam, can I see you?" asked Duncan.

"I don't want to talk, Duncan."

"What if this is the last...I mean, I just want you to know I love you."

Pam clutched the rail of the bed with her left hand.

"I love you too, Duncan. I just don't want to look at you right now."

The surgeons entered the room, and prepared to move Pam to the operating room. The younger doctor stared intensely at his wife. Duncan watched silently, as the bed was whisked past him. He barely had a chance to touch Pam's wrist before they were down the hallway. One of the doctors followed her into the operating room. He had waited outside the door until Pam's argument with her husband was finished. Once Duncan had departed, he spoke to the patient.

"Don't worry, Ms. Fontain. I'll take good care of you. My name is Doctor Percival, but you can call me Preston."

"Oh," said Pam. Alright, Doctor Preston."

"No, just Preston is fine. I'm fully aware of my position," he said, smiling at Pam.

Doctor Percival was a tall, athletic man, seeming too young to be a doctor. He maintained his mousse-filled, spiked hair. He promptly covered his head.

"You're gonna do the surgery?" asked Pam.

"Sure I am, Ms. Fontain," he responded, putting on his rubber gloves.

"Aren't you a little...well you know...I mean...?"

"You mean, a little young, right?"

Pam became cautious before her response.

"I'm thirty-six years old, Ms. Fontain. I've been a doctor for twelve years, and I'm well qualified."

"Oh, I'm sorry Doctor," said Pam.

"You don't have to apologize, Ms. Fontain. I'm used to people thinking I'm too young for my position, but I've earned every piece of recognition I've received. I assure you, I'm the most qualified doctor in this region. If you're not comfortable with me, I could get suggest someone else to perform the surgery, Ms. Fontain."

His eyes seemed to stare at Pam's heart. She felt both comfortable and uneasy with his presence.

"I know you'll do all you can to help me, Preston."

"Thank you, Ms. Fontain."

"You keep calling me Ms. Fontain. It's Mrs. Fontain. Oh, just call me Pam."

He softly touched Pam's cheek.

"Don't worry, Pam. I'll take good care of you."

The nurse walked into the room.

"Doctor, everything is prepared," she said.

"Thank you, Amy."

Seeing the doctor touching Pam's cheek, Amy rolled her eyes and left the room. She slammed the door behind her. She whispered a message to another nurse. They both looked through the windows, snickering at the interaction, before heading toward the coffee machine in the break room.

Doctor Steve Bradley and Doctor Mark Hammonds entered to provide assistance to Doctor Percival. As Pam prepared to go under, her last memories before the gas took effect were the piercing blue eyes of Preston. Preston's involvement in the process was the most prevalent of the three surgeons. He remained completely focused on Pam, and she could see him smile at her even through the mask. The other doctors merely shook their heads at Preston's actions. Once reality disappeared, Pam's surgery began. She could feel the slight poking inside her head. After she regained her senses, the fullness of her pain came forward. The surgery lasted five hours, with Pam sedated for more than eight hours. Some additional sedatives eased her trauma. The nurse walked in with her arms filled with flowers, cards, and balloons meant for Pamela.

"I'll take that for you," said Preston.

"Thanks so much, doctor," said the nurse. "I almost dropped all this stuff. For some reason it has been sitting behind the counter for a few days."

She handed the gifts to Preston, who briskly began organizing them. While Pam was sedated, Preston took all of the small cards attached to the flowers Pam received and replaced them with his own personal cards. The larger Hallmark cards sent by her caring friends, family, and coworkers were put underneath his paperwork to be discarded at a later time. Once again, Preston's blue eyes were the first clear image she saw when she awakened.

"I noticed you didn't have flowers from anyone, so I got these for you," said Preston.

"Thank you, Preston," she replied.

She was caught in between sadness and being grateful for the doctor's kindness. Dazed, Pam attempted to smile and reached to touch the petals of the nearest bouquet. She fell asleep before she could make contact.

Chapter 4

For six hours, Duncan waited in the visitor's room until one of the surgeons approached him.

"Mr. Fontain, we're all done."

"How did it go?" Duncan asked.

"She's doing fine. It was a pretty extensive operation, but we were able to reconnect the arteries and remove the damaged tissue. It's still up in the air concerning how the brain will heal, but the human body is pretty resourceful. We'll keep her here a couple of days. After that, she'll be able to come home. There's not much more we can do for her."

"That's good news, right Doc?"

"That's great news, considering how she came to us. You won't be able to see her until tomorrow. She won't be in any condition to talk to you until then."

"I have to wait until tomorrow?"

"Yes sir," replied the doctor. Go home and get some rest. You can see her after 10:00 am."

Exhausted, Duncan never left the parking structure. He slept in his truck until a service vehicle interrupted his sleep with its' backup signal. The clock on the dash board read 1:17 pm. He rushed back into the hospital and through

Pam's door. Pam was still resting, while the nurse was setting up her post surgery breakfast.

"You'll have to keep it down," said the nurse. She raised her index finger, pressing it against her lips. The top of Pam's head was wrapped with bandages, but most of her facial scars had begun to heal. As Duncan crouched down, Pam slowly opened her eyes.

"It's good to see you," said Duncan.

"I've been awake all morning," Pam replied. "Did you go home or something? I thought you weren't going to leave me."

"I stayed here...Really, I was here. I just slept in the car. I wanted to be here when you woke up, but I guess you were already awake. I'm sorry."

Duncan slapped his forehead, while Pam rolled over to the far side of the bed.

"Sweetie, I said I was sorry," said Duncan.

Pam merely sighed. Duncan retreated to the thinly cushioned chair next to Pam, and remained in that position throughout the night. His chaffed hand was placed against Pam's back. Pam reached back and covered his hand with her own.

The two officers entered the room and approached Pamela. A third officer stood next to Duncan.

"Mr. Fontain, we'll have to ask you to leave the room for a minute. Officer McGomery will escort you out. Duncan followed the Lieutenant's orders. Lieutenant Douglass sat in the seat next to Pamela.

"How are you feeling, Mrs. Fontain?"

"I'm doing alright," she replied.

"I know you probably don't want to deal with the report right now, but we have to follow procedures. We've recreated the accident scene, but there are still some things that don't add up."

"I don't know how much I'll be able to help you," said Pam. "I can't remember too much of anything that happened."

Lieutenant Douglass patted Pam on the wrist.

"I completely understand, Mrs. Fontain. Just tell me what you remember, and we'll try to put the puzzle together."

"Well, I remember driving down the road. The road was pretty slick from the rain. I got lost somewhere around Saso County. I tried to follow the car in front of me back to a main road, but I guess I didn't make it. I remember crashing into a ditch. That's all I remember."

"Do you remember what kind of car you were following?"

"It was too dark to tell. I just followed their tail lights."

"Was anyone following you?"

"I don't think so. How bad was the accident?"

Lieutenant Douglass pulled some photos out of his folder.

"This is what your car looked like right after they pulled you out."

"Oh my God," said Pam.

The car's roof was peeled away from the frame, and the only distinguishable part of the vehicle was the one remaining tire. "Your car was in four pieces, and they found one of your tires about eighty feet away from the wreck. You're very lucky to be alive."

"I know, Lieutenant. I wish I knew exactly what happened."

"So do I Mrs. Fontain. I'll continue to work on this until we piece everything together. If you remember anything, give me a call.

Three day had passed, when the couple finally received more substantial information. As the sun reached its highest point, Doctor Bradley reentered the room.

"Good morning," said the Doctor.

"Hey, Doctor," replied Duncan.

Pam rolled over, sitting up to face Doctor Bradley.

"You don't have to move, Pam. I just want to check your sutures for inflammation or any excessive bleeding."

He slowly removed Pam's bloodied bandages. Noticing Duncan was staring at her wounds, Pamela began to cry. While she held her hand over her eyes, Duncan quickly rubbed her shoulder, looking away from the suture. The doctor parted her hair in various places, from the middle area to the back of her head. Checking her head from all angles, he recorded information. Later, a cat scan was performed on Pam. After the process was completed and the results came back, the doctor returned to address the couple.

"Well, we have good news and bad news."

Pam wiped the tears from her face.

"What's the good news, doctor?" Duncan asked.

"The good news is everything seems to be healing appropriately. There are some things we won't know for a while, but to this point have guarded optimism about your recovery."

"So, what's the bad news?" asked Pam.

"The bad news is you won't be keeping us company anymore. I'm giving permission for your

discharge. As much as I'd like to keep you under
our direct care, policy dictates we keep patients
the minimal amount of time. Most of your
recovery will be in the form of therapy, and the
natural healing process. We will continue to
monitor you, and perform tests to ensure your
recovery, but it would serve no purpose to keep
you here. You can get the same results at home."

Doctor Bradley moved closer to Duncan and
Pam. It'll save you two some money, too," he
whispered. "We all know how expensive hospital
visits can get. Not that I mind the overtime."

Before Pam was released, the nurses
rewrapped her dressing and helped Duncan escort
her to his vehicle. Pam sat with her head down,
while Duncan pushed her wheelchair. Tears
flowed down her face, as the car pulled away from
the hospital.

Days after the surgery, Duncan and Pamela
continued to treat each other cordially, yet each
remained suspicious of their partner. They had
been in their home less than a week, when their
telephone began to constantly ring. It rang more
than twenty times, as Pam was in no mood to
answer. She tried to wait for Duncan to return
from the grocery store, but the ringing became
unbearable. Rolling over to the right side of the
mattress, Pam answered.

"Who is this," she shouted.

"Pamela, this is Preston."

"I don't know any Preston," said Pam.

"It's Doctor Percival."

"Doctor Percival? I thought you were on a
vacation or something?"

"I am, but I told you I'd make sure you
were doing alright."

"I'm doing a little better, but I still can't feel my hand. I'm still glad you called."

"I thought you'd like it," said Preston.

"Excuse me," said Pam, curiously.

"I try to make sure my patients are taken care of even after they're out of my care. It's just a little personal policy of mine."

"Well, I really appreciate you calling, but I'm a little tired."

"Oh, I understand, Pam. I need to get back to the woods, anyway. I hope I didn't disturb you too much. I'm just concerned about you. I heard the argument between you and your husband. It sounds like you're having some difficulties in your relationship."

"I don't know if I feel comfortable discussing my relationship with my doctor."

"Don't think of me as a doctor," Preston replied. "Think of me as a friend. Besides, I have a degree in medical psychology, so helping patients in their personal lives isn't foreign to me. I know you don't need a stressful relationship stalling your recovery."

"I don't want to talk about this now," said Pamela.

"I understand completely. I just want you to know I'm there whenever you need me."

"That's so sweet, Doctor Percival."

"Preston, remember?"

"I'm sorry...Preston."

"Pam, if you ever want to talk, or if you experience any discomfort from your surgery, give me a call. The nurse gave you my cell phone number, didn't she?"

"I think it's on my paperwork," Pam answered.

"You can call me at any time."

"I'll keep that in mind, Doctor."

"Preston, remember?"

"I'll keep that in mind, Preston."

"I'll be in touch with you soon. Take care, Pam."

"You too, Preston," said Pam.

Duncan walked in while Pam was ending her conversation. He noticed her mood had changed noticeably since the time he left.

"So who was that?"

"Oh, it wasn't anybody special. It was just the doctor."

"What did he say?"

"He didn't say too much. He was just checking on my condition."

"He's checking on you already? It ain't even been a week yet," said Duncan.

"Duncan, don't start with me. I'm too tired to deal with this."

Duncan paused and took a deep breath.

"Alright, I'm sorry for overreacting. I just got a bad feeling about that guy."

One week later, Pam received another call from Professor Wembly.

"Pamela, I'm glad I got a hold of you. I heard what happened with your accident. Are you feeling any better?"

"I'm feeling a little better, Professor," Pam replied. "I just wish the recovery had gone a little faster. I just want to be normal again."

"Be patient, my dear. Everything will work out. Did you get the cards I sent you?"

"You sent cards to me? I guess something happened to them. It doesn't matter. It's the thought that counts."

"That's true, Pamela. Since you're doing better, I guess I might as well give you some good news."

"What news is that?" Pam asked

"There were a number of people who wanted to buy your sculpture. Unfortunately, there was no way to keep up with Mr. Adam's bidding. Anyone who knows Mr. Adams knows what he wants, he gets. I have four potential buyers that are willing to purchase whatever you create for a significant amount of money. Your work has become a 'must have' in the art community."

"I don't know if I can create sculptures anymore. I'm still not completely healed from the accident."

"Don't think that I don't understand your condition. When you're ready, the buyers will be ready. They realize Rome wasn't created in a day. Just take your time and get well."

"I truly appreciate your help, Professor."

"I'm always there to help you. I'm sure those doctor bills aren't going away by themselves. Just call me when you get have a piece completed."

Pam began to look at the four unfinished pieces she had yet to mold. Her right hand hadn't regained its strength, yet she longed to work on her project. Slow and deliberately, she rolled across the mattress, trying to reach her clay. She moved one step away from the bed, became lightheaded, and collapsed to the floor. Crying, she pounded her hand against the hardwood floor. Duncan rushed into the room and kneeled down beside Pam.

"What happened?" he asked.

"I'm sick of this bed," Pam answered. "I'm sick and tired of feeling like a vegetable. I can't even work on my sculptures because of my hand."

"Ain't there anything the doctor can do?"

"Damn if I know," she replied.

Pam started crying. Duncan stared at the digital clock sitting on top of the dresser.

"Do you want me to stay home from work?"

Pam shook her head.

"If you have to ask, then you should leave."

"I'm just asking. Why do you have to make an argument out of everything?"

"I don't need this, Duncan," said Pam. "Just go to work."

Duncan stood in disbelief, with his hands on the top of his head. On his way out, the downstairs phone rang.

"Who is it?" he yelled.

There was only silence.

"Hello...," he shouted.

There was still no response. Duncan slammed the phone on to its base and left the house. Soon after, the phone rang again. After the fourth ring, Pamela was able to reach the phone. She cleared her throat and held the receiver to her head.

"Hello," said Pam in a raspy voice.

"Yes, um...Mrs. Fontain, this is Sarah from the Quincy Wellness Center. I'm calling on behalf of Doctor Percival. The doctor would like to see you to check on your progress. Do you think you'd be available tomorrow at 2:00 pm?"

"I don't know," Pam replied. "I have to check with my husband. I don't know if I'll have a way to get there. I still can't use my hand, and my car is still totaled."

The phone became quiet, with only the rustling of papers heard from Sarah's end of the telephone.

"Hello," said Pamela.

"Oh, I'm sorry Ma'am. You'll have to excuse me. This is my first week. I'm just checking the doctor's schedule to see if there are any other times available. I'll schedule you for that 2:00 pm appointment, and you can let me know if we need to make any changes. I'm sure the doctor will move things around for you."

"Who should I ask for?" Pam asked.

"Well, my name's Sarah. I'm pretty sure you can ask for me or any of our other people...I mean associates can help you."

After a long day of work, Duncan walked out to his truck in the company parking lot. He stood in amazement of the condition of his truck. All four of his tires were flat, with large gashes in his tires. The hood of his truck had a large drawing of lip prints written in lip stick. In the center of the picture was a small teddy bear with its head cut off. Looking closer, he found a business card. Written on the back, a message said, "Payback's a bitch." He stuck the card in his back pocket and continued to assess the damage.

Duncan kicked the side of his car and returned to the human resource office.

"Somebody trashed my car," he shouted.

"Would you like me to call the police?" said the manager.

"Hell yeah, you can call the police."

After waiting more than twenty minutes, Duncan finally spotted the police squad car. Two officers stepped out of the vehicle. As they moved closer, Duncan noticed they were the officers who had approached him at the hospital.

"So we meet again, Mr. Fontain," said Lieutenant Douglass.

"Did they have to send you two again?" Duncan asked.

Officer Davis walked up close to Duncan, stopping inches away from his face.

"What kind of trouble did you get yourself in this time, tubby?"

Duncan balled his hand and stared at the small officer.

"Mr. Fontain; I wouldn't even think about doing anything if I were you," said the Lieutenant, with his hand on the butt of his gun. "Would you like to file a report?"

"Of course I would. Somebody messed up my truck. It ain't even paid off, yet."

Officer Davis took out his pad, and began recording the statement.

"Do you have any idea who might have been responsible for this?"

"Yeah, I got an idea. There's this woman who used to work with me. We got into a little argument and I know she's got issues with me."

"What is the name of this woman?"

Duncan paused for a second.

"You know what, officer? It's not really that serious."

"Sir is there something you don't want to tell us about this woman?" asked the officer.

"I just don't want to start any trouble with her. She's already caused enough problems in my life."

The lieutenant patted Duncan on the back and pointed to his vehicle.

"It looks like your trouble isn't going away any time soon, buddy."

He whispered in Duncan's ear.

"I've seen situations like this before. This woman wants to send you a message, and if you don't want more things like this to happen to you, you need to let us help you."

Officer Davis stepped in front of Duncan.

"If you want a psycho chick doing stuff like this over and over, that's your business. Next time leave us outta your drama."

Lieutenant Douglass put his hand on the officer's chest.

"I got this under control, Davis," he said. "Mr. Fontain, just tell us about the person you think committed this vandalism."

"Her name is Sierra Dimaano. We worked on a project together. We had a little argument over an incident a couple months ago."

The Lieutenant continued to record Duncan's statement.

"Was this incident concerning a sexual nature, Mr. Fontain?"

"No sir," exclaimed Duncan. "I didn't do anything with her. I mean...I thought about it, but I ain't screwin around on my wife. Maybe that's why she was mad at me."

"Wait a minute," screamed Officer Davis. "Does this have anything to do with your wife's accident?"

"Hell no," Duncan responded. "It was those damn no good tires. We had to pay so many bills I thought I could get by without changing them. I guess I was wrong."

"Are you sure, Mr. Fontain?"

"Yeah, I'm sure. She might have messed up my truck, but I don't think she had anything to do with that situation. I'm just glad my wife is alive."

Duncan sat on the hood of his car, wiping the tears from his face.

"You don't have to start crying. I think you've been through enough this night," said the lieutenant. "I'll file the report and we'll see if we can fill in the blanks. We can give you a ride home if you need it."

"That's alright, officer. My buddy Donald gets off in a little while. He'll drop me off."

"I hope you have a better night, Mr. Fontain," said Lieutenant Douglass.

"Just do me a favor and try not to get killed," added Officer Davis.

"Whatever you say, officer," Duncan replied.

Chapter 5

Sylvia talked to Pam, as she drove her to her appointment.

"So, what's this Doctor Percival like."

"Oh, he's alright," said Pam. "He's just a doctor, you know?"

"Pam, who do you think you're talking to? Is he cute?"

"Well, he's very handsome. He looks so young too, but I have no interest in him."

"What if you weren't with Duncan? Would you have any interest then?" Sylvia asked. She nudged Pam on her shoulder.

"Girl, you are a mess," said Pam. "I'm not going to even let your little mind wander by answering that question."

There was silence, until the two women made eye contact with one another. When each of the friends was unable to hold their giggling, both burst out laughing.

As they reached their destination, Sylvia and Pam walked to the waiting room. When the nurse called Pam's name, they exchanged another smile.

"Have fun playing doctor," said Sylvia.

After being escorted into another room, Pamela waited for the doctor to arrive. Preston slowly entered the room.

"How are we doing?" he asked.

He leaned over and softly kissed Pam on the side of her cheek. Holding his checklist under his arm, Preston sat next to Pamela.

"I guess I'm doing a little better," she replied. "I'm still having trouble with my hand."

"Are you having moments where you hand goes numb."

"I hardly ever have feeling in my hand."

"It's not abnormal to have a loss of sensation after your accident."
Preston pulled a soft blue rubber ball out of one of his dresser drawers. He placed the ball in Pam's hand.

"I want you to try squeezing this ball as much as you can, Pam."

Pam didn't completely understand the reasoning behind the doctor's request, yet she complied. She gripped the ball, squeezing it within her palm. Pam's muscles throbbed with pain, but she continued to squeeze. After more than fifteen minutes, the pain in her hand began to subside.

"You're doing very well, Pam. You just need to regain your strength in the muscles you haven't used in a while."

Preston wrapped his hand around Pam's hand.

"I want you to continue to use this exercise whenever you have moments of free time. It may not look like much, but this will definitely help you with your recovery."
Pam was pleased to hear the doctor's compliment pertaining to her performance, yet she failed to show any enthusiasm.

"You should be pleased, Pam," said Preston.

"I am pleased, Preston."

"So what's wrong?"

"I don't know if I should say it or not," said Pam.

"It's alright, Pam. You can tell me what's on your mind."

Preston moved a chair close to Pam and sat in front of her.

"I just wanted to tell you about something that happened last night. I had a flashback or a nightmare or something. I don't know if it was the drugs messing with my mind, or what. All I know is that while I was sleeping, I could see the accident. I saw what happened with me. Somebody tried to kill me."

"Did you call the police?"

"I don't know if they'd believe me. I don't think my own husband would believe me, so why would the police? Maybe I'm just going crazy, but I could see what happened."

"Did you try to tell him?"

"No, he left for work before I woke up. I just needed to tell somebody before my memory starts acting up."

"You know you can tell me anything, honey," said Preston. "What happened?"

"It was raining pretty hard, and I was driving down a dark road. I remember someone crashing into me from behind."

Pam began to cry, as Preston massaged her shoulders.

"I saw these women in a red truck. I screamed for them to help me...but they hit me again."

"Do you know any of these women?"
Preston asked.

"I don't think so. I really don't remember
the whole incident. I just remember the bits and
pieces from the nightmare."

"I could help you out with your memory,"
said Preston. "Have you ever heard of hypnosis?"

"I've heard of it, but I never thought it
really worked," Pam responded.

"Studies have shown when hypnosis is used
in combination with mental relaxation, powerful
recall can be quickly developed. It is very
effective in allowing an individual to overcome
mental blocks. It's all about guiding patients into
a state to relieve thoughts, feelings, or
experiences."

"Do I have to look at your pocket watch or
something?"

"No Pam, you've been watching too many
made for TV movies. That's not how we operate in
medical hypnosis. It's all about relaxation of mind
and body. I just   want you to lay back, relax and
concentrate on a peaceful setting. Count slowly
from one to one hundred."

Pam lay back on the table and began to
slowly count as the doctor requested. Though she
doubted the reality of hypnotism, her mind began
to wander and rest in a dreamlike state. By the
time she reached the count of eighty, Pam was
fully hypnotized.

"Can you hear me Pam?"

"Yes Preston," she replied.

"I want you to try to remember the
accident. Its cold and the rain is falling. Can you
feel the rain?"

"Yes, I can feel it. It's so cold. I can't see
anything."

"Can you see any vehicles around you?"

"Not really. There are some headlights behind me."

"What are you doing?"

"I'm trying to get their attention. They're pulling up next to me. I can see the truck. It's red and it has tinted windows. It's moving closer to me. Nooooooo..."

Pamela screamed and twisted in the seat. The doctor grabbed her by her wrists to restrain her.

"Pam, its OK," said Preston.

He clapped his hands together, creating a crisp noise. It snapped Pam's hypnotic state abruptly.

"It's alright Pam."

Preston held her close, until she remained calm.

"Were you able to see the women in the truck?"

"Yes, I saw them," said Pam, wiping the tears from her eyes.

"What did they look like?"

"There was one that was black. She was light skinned with long braids in her hair. The other one was PueterRican. She was a small woman with gold highlights in her dark hair."

"I thought you said there were three women."

"There were three women, but I'm having trouble remembering the third one."

"I need you to concentrate, Pam. What did she look like?"

"I remember something about her eyes. They were sort of Asian looking eyes. Yeah, she was mixed with Chinese or something. I can't remember her hair color, but I know it was dark."

Pam slapped the both sides of her face with her the palms of her hands.

"Wait a minute...the one with the dark hair. Her name was Sara. No, it wasn't Sara. Her name was Sierra. She had an affair with my husband."

"That name sounds really familiar." Preston's lips curled like a wolf discovering his prey.

"Sierra, huh," he whispered.

"Yes, her name was Sierra."

"Your husband cheated on you? How could he do something like that to a woman like you?" Preston pulled Pam close to him.

"He has no idea how many men would kill to have a woman like you."

"Oh yeah...Tell him that."

"So, these women hit you?"
"I think so," Pam replied.

"Don't worry about any of that. I'll take care of it," said Preston.

"Do you think the police would believe you if you told them what happened?" she asked.

"Pam, I told you not to worry. I'll take care of it. I want you to take it easy and rest. If you need anything, and I mean anything, just call me. OK?"

"Thank you so much, Preston. It's nice to have someone I can turn to."

"I know, Pam. I feel like I've known you for a long time. I think this is the beginning of something special."

"I think I better get home. My friend is still out there waiting for me in the lobby. I'll talk to you soon."

"See you soon, honey," Preston replied.

Later that night, Duncan returned from work. He walked up the stairs to find Pamela sharpening her dull art supplies.

"How's it going, Pam?" he asked.
"I've been waiting to talk to you all day. I had the craziest nightmare last night."

"What was it about?"

"It was about the accident. I think I saw what happened."

Duncan's hung his head.

"I'm so sorry I didn't change those tires, baby."

He sat on the bed next to Pam.

"No Duncan, that's not what I'm talking about. I think someone cause my accident."

"Who do you think did it?"

"I think it was that broad named Sierra," Pam replied.

"Oh, here we go again. I thought we were trying to get over that situation. I'm doing everything I can to show you that you can trust me, and you keep bringing her up."

"Are you even listening to me? This is not about you sleeping with her. I'm trying to tell you that I think she ran me off the road."

"Are you sure it was her. Maybe you just want it to be her. You probably think we're messing around now, and want her to go to jail."

Pam stood up from the bed, and pointed her finger in Duncan's face.

"I told you that I'm not talking about you and her. I saw her and some other women in my dream hit me with their truck."

"You're sure about this?" asked Duncan

"Duncan, the truck was red, and the women looked me right in the face. Maybe I'm going crazy, I don't know."

"Do you want to tell the police about it?"

"Not if they act same as you. I don't want to go through this again."

Duncan grabbed his wife's hand.

"I don't know how to tell you this, but something happened to the truck."

"What do you mean by something happened to our truck?"

"Somebody slashed the tires and wrecked the hood."

Pam crossed her arms and glared at Duncan.

"Somebody like who?" asked Pam.

"I don't know. It could have been some kids messing around."

"Or it could have been Sierra. I don't want to deal with this drama for the rest of my life, Duncan."

Duncan sprang to his feet.

"Do you think I want to deal with it? I don't even know if it was Sierra."

"So now you want to cover up for her. You can pretend all you want, but you know she did it. Where is the truck?"

"I called a tow truck to bring it here, until I figure out what to do with it. It's pretty messed up. They're going to use a flatbed to tow it."

"How did you get here?"

"I got a ride home from Donald."

"You better make sure that woman doesn't touch any more of our things, Duncan."

Aggravated, Duncan grabbed a beer out of the refrigerator and stormed downstairs into the partially finished basement. As he continued to sip his beer, Duncan began arranging his bright orange and camouflage paraphernalia for his hunting trip planned for the next day. Hearing the noise in the basement, Pamela roamed down the steps.

"Duncan, what are you doing?"

"I'm getting ready for my trip tomorrow," he replied.

"Have you lost your mind? You're still planning to go on that damn hunting trip, with all the stuff that's going on."

"Dammit, Pam, I'm stressed out. If I don't get away, I'm gonna say something or do something I'll regret. You know how long I've planned to go on the trip."

"Of course I know, but I thought you would stay around while all these crazy things were happening."

"I'm sorry honey, but I'm stressed out. I know you've been through a lot of drama, but so have I. I just need to get away for awhile."

"Fine Duncan, go ahead. I'm not going to stop you. You leave every time I need you."

She ran back up the stairs and slammed the door to their bedroom. Frustrated, Duncan rested on the tattered old sofa in the basement. Through the night, Duncan and Pamela slept in separate parts of their home. Both were awaken by the continuous honking of a horn outside the house. Duncan peered through the dusty basement window, barely able to see the bottom of Donald's Ford Explorer. He grabbed his gun bag, along with a bag containing his necessities for the weekend. Duncan jogged up the steps and moved toward the bottom of the stairs leading to their bedroom.

"Pamela," he called. "Honey, I'm getting ready to leave."

Slowly, Pam approached Duncan. She stopped at the top of the steps. She stood with her arms crossed, shaking her head.

"So you're still going? Well, have a good time."

Pam moved back toward the room.

"Pam, wait," screamed Duncan.

"I really need to go. I might not even stay the whole weekend. It'll give you some time to work on your project."

Donald repeatedly honked the horn.

"Your friend is waiting for you," said Pam.

"You better go."

Duncan dropped his bags and walked upstairs. He attempted to kiss Pam on the lips, but she tuned her head to allow his lips to merely touch her cheek.

"I left the number to Donald's cell phone so you can reach me if there's an emergency."

"Goodbye Duncan," said Pam.

When Duncan closed the door, Pam latched the chain behind him.

Later in the day, Pam called Sylvia at her office.

"Hey girl, how are you?" asked Pam.

"Girl, they got me working like a Hebrew slave. Ever since you left, I've had to work late everyday."

"I'm so sorry, Sylvia."

"Oh girl, it's not your fault. You did what you had to do. If I had your talent, I would have done the same thing. So what's going on?"

"I just needed someone to talk to."

"Pam, I wish I could talk to you. I really miss you, but I can't talk right now. The boss has been on me all week and I can't afford to lose this job."

"I understand," said Pam, softly.

"Don't get all sad on me. I'll give you a call as soon as I get a chance."

After her conversation with Sylvia, Pam searched for another friend to call. Grabbing her therapeutic ball, Pam began to rapidly squeeze it.

After a few moments, she settled on calling Doctor Percival.

"Doctor Percival," said Preston.

"Hello Preston, this is Pam."

"How are you doing, Pam."

"I'm doing alright. I'm sorry to call you on your cell phone, but I needed someone to talk to. I can call you another time if you're too busy to talk."

"I'm never too busy to speak with you," Preston responded. "Where's your guy at?"

"He went hunting up north," replied Pam.

"You mean he left you at home by yourself? As much as I love hunting, there's no way I would have left a woman like you alone."

"I'm sorry Preston. I probably shouldn't have called you."

"Look Pam, I told you that you could call me anytime you wanted to."

The telephone connection between the two became muddled.

"It's hard to hear you Preston. Where are you?"

"I'm at my cabin. It's hard to keep a connection here. I don't think I'll be here too long. I have a lot of things I need to get out of the way."

"I know, Preston. I'm sorry I bothered you."

"No, it's alright Pam. I told you that you could call me anytime. By the way, what's your husband wearing?"

"He's probably wearing his camouflage coat. It says 'Big Game' on the back. He paid over

three hundred dollars for that ugly coat. It even has a picture of a dead deer on the back."
"Well, I'll make sure I say hello if I see him up here. I'll talk to you soon."

Chapter 6

Duncan and Donald arrived at the woods in Northern Wisconsin early Saturday morning.

As they exited Donald's truck, Duncan took a deep breath of the cool fresh air.

"Now this is what I'm talking about, Duncan," he said. "You don't know how long I've been waiting to get out here and enjoy this."

"Me too," said Donald, pulling his bag out of the cab of the Ford.

They set their belongings inside Donald's small rented cabin. Anxious to begin their hunting trip, the men headed out into the woods in search of deer. Sporting his 'Big Game' coat, Duncan buckled his leather sheath to his thick belt and inserted his hunting knife. He carried a long 30-06 rifle. Donald was dressed in a bright fluorescent orange vest, which covered his tan coveralls. He toted a dual trigger, double barrel muzzleloader rifle, complete with hollow point bullets. They walked side by side, each with their weapon prepared to claim their bounty.

"Man, I love that coat. When are you gonna let me wear it?" asked Donald.

"Ain't gonna happen," laughed Duncan.

"There's only room for one 'Big Game'."

"You might be bigger than me, but nobody gets bigger game than me," said Donald.

"Do you wanna bet?"
Donald smiled.

"I'll give you the first shot at a deer. If you can't take him down with one shot, I get to wear your coat for the rest of the weekend."

"So what happens when I take him down?" asked Duncan.

"Aren't we cocky? Alright, 'Big Game'. If you take him down, I'll pay to have its head mounted. Do we have a bet?"
Duncan shook Donald's hand.

"Yeah, we have a bet. I already have a place picked out for it."

Through the woods, the two men slowly walked. Upon hearing a rustling on the leaves, they stopped it their tracks. Less than fifty feet away stood a whitetail buck. Its powerful muscles ripple underneath the deer's brownish red fur. The buck's nose sniffled through the white fur surrounding his mouth. Incredibly large 22 point antlers gave away the deer's position. Out of the corner of their eyes, the hunters watched the deer. Donald let Duncan move forward, laying ten steps behind his friend. Confidently and carefully, Duncan aimed his rifle at the deer. As he pulled the trigger, the blast of the .44 caliber bullet streamed straight toward the deer. In an instance, the buck dashed deeper into the woods.

"I got him, didn't I?" asked Duncan.

"I don't think so, man."

They walked toward the spot where the deer previously stood. A tree with a large bullet hole provided evidence Duncan had missed.

"Alright, give it up," said Donald, dancing around the tree.

"Damn, I thought I had him."
Duncan removed his coat.

"You better not get it dirty," said Duncan.

"You better not get it dirty," sarcastically mocked Donald. "Don't worry, I won't mess up your coat, but I will show you how to bring down the real 'Big Game'. You've been hunting those little does so long, you have no idea how these bucks operate. Watch and learn."

Donald switched places with his companion.

"We call this circle driving the deer. Do you smell that?"

"Yeah, what's that smell?" asked Duncan.

"That's the odor of the deer when they're scared. We must be around the one that ran away. I want you to go over to that tree and start grunting."

Donald point to a tree nearly thirty feet away.

"Why the hell should I do that?"

"When the buck hears you, he'll run toward me. I'll be over on top of that hill. After that, it's bye bye Bambi."

"Whatever you say, Donald. If you miss, I want my coat back."

"It's a deal," said Donald. "Just get your ass over there before he leaves."

Duncan quietly jogged over toward the tree and began to grunt. As he made the noises, the rustling started again. The deer bolted out of the brush and straight toward the direction of Donald. Peering through his telescopic sight, Donald focused on the buck. The powerful gun rested on his shoulder, while he patiently held one of the two triggers. Duncan waived at his fellow hunter, signaling the deer's movement. Donald clutched the first trigger, and the blast of the hollow point bullet rammed into the flesh of the massive buck. Grasping the second trigger of the muzzleloader, he refocused his aim through the scope. As he was set to fire, a blast of pain entered his chest. While the deer was slowly dying, Donald's body dropped to the leaf covered woods. Hearing the second shot, Duncan ran toward Donald's location.

"Donald, what happened man," asked Duncan?

Donald crawled along the floor of the wilderness, coughing and gasping. Surveying the landscape, Duncan searched for the pathway leading to the shooter. He held his rifle, prepared to fire at the killer. Continuing to aim at the woods, Duncan dropped to one knee and checked the pulse of his friend. His eyes jumped in every direction, but no one was in site. There was a hole in the left side of his jacket, which blood flowed from. Donald's chest rose and sunk with each passing moment. Reaching inside Donald's pocket, Duncan pulled out the cell phone and called for help. Within minutes, the local Sheriff's department arrived. Donald failed to give evidence of any life remaining within him. The area became a crime scene, and Donald's body was draped with a large black tarp. For hours, Duncan was questioned by a number of officers. After gathering the evidence and finding no witnesses, the men came to the conclusion that the shooting was accidental. A black Lexus SUV left the woods, and headed toward the highway.

Preston arrived at the hospital and headed toward his office. His presence, as well as his attire was a surprise to the receptionist. He was dressed in a brown kaki shirt with faded blue jeans.

"Back from your trip so soon, Doctor Percival," asked the receptionist.

"I just had to take care of some things, but I'm still off the clock, Debbie," he answered.

"Just let me know if you need anything, Doctor."
Debbie smiled at the doctor, looking him up and down as he walked down the hallway.
Preston barely paid any attention to her offer. Entering his office, Preston noticed his secretary on the outside of the desk, organizing papers. As he walked past her, Preston softly brushed against her back.

"Oh, hello Doctor Percival. I wasn't expecting you today. Did you have a good vacation?"

"Of course, Sarah. I just needed to come back to get some things in order."

"Well, I'm glad you made if back safely," said Sarah, politely.
As she turned around, Preston took a long look at her figure. He deviously smiled at her.

"Sarah, could you meet me in the X-ray room for a moment, please?"

"Sure Doctor Percival," she replied.

When she came into the dark room, the doctor shut the door behind her. He was standing in front of some bone X-rays, with the light being the only illumination in the room.

"Sarah, what does this look like to you?" he asked.

"Looks like a hairline fracture in the vertebra."

"That's just what it is, except if you look closely, you can see the weakness in the bone's density."

"Why did you call me in to see this, doctor?"

"I called you in because I think you have more to offer this hospital that just as a secretary. You ever thought about being the head of nursing for this whole wing?"

Sara laughed.

"I've only been here a little while, doctor. I didn't even finish nursing school," she answered.

"That doesn't matter to me. I have a lot of pull in the medical field. It's just a matter of moving a couple things around."

"Is there anything special I have to do?" Sara asked.

Preston moved behind her, wrapping his arms around her waist. He kissed her on the back of her neck. Sarah pulled his interlocked hands away from her waist.

"What are you doing? Sarah asked."

"What do you think I'm doing," Preston responded. "Why do you think I asked you to clear my schedule this week?"

"I can't do this, doctor. I just got engaged."

Preston began to sweat.

"Stop lying to me. I know you're not engaged. I don't know why you're holding back. Don't you know how many women working here would love to be in your position? I guess you don't want to work here."

"You can't fire me for not sleeping with you," said Sarah, adamantly. "That's sexual harassment."

"Don't you know who I am? I can fire whoever I want for whatever I want. Who do you think they'd believe? Do you think they'd believe some girl who flunked out of nursing school and has a baby by a guy in jail, or the best neurosurgeon in the world?"

"You can't do this to me," said Sarah. "There's no reason to let me go."

"I'm sorry Sarah. You did it to yourself. By the way, do you remember the report you were supposed to finish yesterday?"

"I put it on your desk before I left."

"Well I never received it," said Preston. "That was a very important assignment, and you didn't get the job done. I'm going to have to fire you. How is that for a reason?"

"I set that report on your desk at four o'clock," Sarah screamed.

"I'm sorry Sarah, but I have to do what I have to do. We take our responsibilities very serious here."

Preston's cell phone rang. He moved toward the corner of the X-ray room.

"I'll be there in a minute," said Preston. He turned back to Sarah.

"I have to leave, so I expect you to be gone when I get back. Make sure you clean up after yourself. I don't want the new girl to have to start off with a messy desk."

Preston winked and turned the lights on, as he left the room.

Sarah cried, as she packed her belongings into a small cardboard box. When she finished taking her personal items, she remembered all the gifts of appreciation she had given the doctor. Boldly walking into his empty office, Sarah began to dump her gifts into the box, including the custom wood grain clock on the wall, the digital address book, and the "Best Boss in the World" mug.

 While sticking the cup into her box, Sarah discovered a folder with pictures sliding out. She curiously grabbed the first picture. The photo was of a young, dark haired teenage girl on a beach. She was very attractive, but had an uneasy look on her face. Moving through picture after picture of the same girl, the pictures captured her from her teenage years to womanhood. Sarah could see two unique qualities in the pictures. When the girl was facing the camera, she had this sadness that was prevalent in her brown eyes. That look wasn't evident in the photos of the woman as she aged, but she never seemed to be facing the camera. Some of those pictures were taken with her walking in the mall, sitting in the park, or undressing in front of the curtains. In many of the pictures, the people beside her were cut out. There were more than seventy pictures of her.

 Sarah looked out the glass to make sure no one was coming. She put one of the pictures in her pocket. Underneath the file of pictures were photos of another woman. The similarities were striking, especially the features of this woman in comparison to the pictures of the other as a teenager. Sarah knew the woman looked familiar, but couldn't identify her until she found the medical report underneath the pictures. "Pamela Fontain," she said quietly. There were several photos of Pam, from her medical photos to pictures that seemed to be cut out of her old high school year book. All of her information was within the file, with a complete listing of Duncan's work schedule, Pamela's appointment schedule, and some other unfamiliar names of three other women.

She took whatever she could carry, photocopying as much as she could in a short period. Sarah grabbed one of the pictures of Pam, before attempting to arrange all the folders in the order they were in before she entered. She quickly left the office, and rushed to her car. She raced home, and snatched the telephone from the wall. Taking Pam's number out of her pocket, Sarah called her at home.

The telephone rang twice, before Pam answered.

"Mrs. Fontain, this is Sarah from Quincy," she said, breathing heavily.

"Hello Sarah. How are you?"

"Um...I'm alright, I guess. Have you talked to Doctor Percival today?"

"Yes, I just called him a little while before you called. I'm just waiting for him to call me back."

"I'm glad I caught you before he called you."

The other line on Pam's end of the telephone began to beep.

"Hold on a second Sarah."

She clicked over to the second line.

"Hello?"

"Hey Pam, this is Preston. I called you as soon as I could."

"Thanks for returning my call, Preston. I just called because the medicine you gave me is causing me problems. I've been feeling sick to my stomach lately, and I'm constantly drowsy. Is there anything else you can prescribe?"

"There are a few options we can pursue. The first one is probably the best. I can prescribe you a psycho stimulant that would stop both your pain and bring back some of your energy. You still don't have a way to get to the office, do you?"

"No, Preston. We still haven't gotten my car fixed," Pam replied.

"I told you I would take care of you, didn't I? I guess the doctor is going to have to make a house call."

"A house call?" Pam asked.

"I won't be long," said Preston, hanging up.

"Hello, Preston?"

Tired of waiting, Sarah hung up and went back to taking care of her son. She called back fifteen minutes later.

"I'm so sorry, Sarah. I was talking to Doctor Percival. What did you want to tell me?"

"I wanted to warn you about some things. I was going through some of the doctor's papers, and I found some of your personal information in his files. I need to see you to show you what I found."

Pam's doorbell rang.
"Hold on a minute, Sarah."

Looking through the glass, Pamela saw Preston on her front porch. She slowly opened the door.

"Preston, I didn't expect you to come so soon."

"Let's just say I was in the neighborhood. I just wanted to give you that prescription."

"Well, let me get off this phone."

Pam turned her back to the doctor.

"Sarah, could you call me back a little later? The doctor just came over to give me a prescription."

"Pam, don't hang up the phone. I need to tell you something."

Barely hearing the conversation, Preston moved close to Pam.

"Did I hear that Sarah is on the phone?" he asked.

Hesitantly, Pam answered.

"Yes, it's your assistant."

"Can I talk to her for a moment, please?"

"I guess, Preston," said Pam.

Grabbing the phone from Pam's hand, Preston spoke loudly.

"Hello Sarah, this is Doctor Percival. Is everything going alright at the office?"

Sarah was silent.

"Good, that's good to hear," said the doctor.

He walked away from Pamela with the telephone, and began to whisper to Sarah.

"Don't you ever call any of my patients without my permission? Why are you calling, anyway? I told you, you don't work for me anymore. If you do anything to disrupt my work, I'll make you wish you never met me. Do you understand me? Your son will never see you again and you'll have a closed casket funeral. Do you understand me?"

"Yes...I understand," said Sarah.
Preston spoke loudly once again.

"That's good, Sarah. I'm glad we cleared that up. Why don't you take the rest of the day off?"

"I hate you," she whispered.

"I'm glad to hear that. Just remember what we talked about, dear. Goodbye."

Preston hung up on Sarah, and handed the phone back to Pamela.

"Is everything alright, Preston?"

"Oh, everything is fine, Pam. We just needed to clear a few things up. I need to get back to the office, but I grabbed a few samples of a prescription for you."

He pulled a small plastic cylinder container out of his jacket.

"This is a psycho stimulant called Dexedrine. It should help you with the pain, and your drowsiness. Take two of these a day."

"Should I still take the other medicine?" asked Pam.

"It's entirely up to you. I doubt you will have any trouble if you take them on a full stomach. To be honest, I don't usually write prescriptions, but I want to make sure you're taken care of."

"I really appreciate that, doctor."

"I know you do, Pam. You'll have ample opportunity to show me your appreciation soon enough, but I need to get back to the office."

He grabbed Pam's hand, kissing her gently on her knuckles.

"I'll see you soon, Pam," said Preston.

He hurried out of the door.

When Preston returned to his office, he immediately realized things weren't as he left them. He counted his pictures one by one.

'Seventy-Eight pictures,' he mumbled. Preston searched frantically for the two missing pictures. Retracing his steps in his mind, the doctor remembered locking his door. No one had access to his office, except...his secretary. Visually scanning the room, he saw the photocopier was left on. He pressed the 'copy' button to see what was the last item copied on the machine. Moments later, scattered pictures of Pamela and

Jenna came from the lone page. Preston kicked the machine, and tucked the page into his briefcase. He rearranged his photos, locking them in a case underneath his desk. After a brief look in his organizer, he stormed to his car. Preston's first stop was at a neighborhood art supplies store.

"Do you have any supplies for sculpting?" Preston asked the clerk.

"Look in isle five," she answered.

Preston bought two gift sets of supplies including professional grade scalpels, tools to add texture, and various other items. One box was put in his trunk, while another was placed in the seat next to him. In the parking lot, Preston opened each item. He stared at the finely crafted scalpel which was lighter, and more provisioned than the one he preformed surgery with. Smiling, he searched through his organizer once again, and drove off. Stopping back at Pam's home, Preston left the gift just below her front door. From his cell phone, Preston called Pam while he drove away from her house.

"Hello," answered Pam.

"Hey Pam, this is Preston again. I just wanted to give you something."

"Preston, you don't have to give me anything. I mean, I appreciate it, but you don't have to do that."

"Sorry baby, it's already done. Look outside your door."

Walking away with the cordless phone in her hand, Pam looked through the window.

"I don't see anything."

"It's outside your door," said Preston.

Pam cracked the door open and saw a box inches away from the door. The professionally

wrapped box had a small card on it. The card read
'just for you'. Bending over to retrieve the gift,
Pam became excited. She noticed the card had
the name of her favorite art supplies store on it.
"What did you get me?" she asked.
        "Just open it," answered Preston.
Ripping the paisley maroon paper off the wooden
box, Pam tried to imagine its contents. Lifting the
lid, she saw an elegant turquoise handled scalpel
along with the top of the line sculpting tools.
        "Wow, I can't believe you got this for me.
It's lovely, but I don't think I can accept this. I
don't think Duncan would like me to have such an
extravagant gift from you."
        "I'm sorry Pam, but I can't take it back.
You know the policy of that type of store," said
Preston, laughing. "You don't have to tell him I
bought it for you. I'm sure he doesn't care about
the talent you have. He might not appreciate your
gifts, but I do. We'll just keep this between me
and you, alright."
Pam smile was evident through the phone line.
        "Well, since you can't take it back, I'll keep
it, but please doctor, no more presents."
        "Sure Pam, whatever you say."
Looking further into the wrapping, Pam found two
silver keys.
        "What are these keys for?" she asked.
        "It's the keys to my home. I figured I'd
make you a copy if you ever needed a place to
relax away from home."
        "Preston, you know I can't accept keys to
your home."
        "You don't need to use them right now
Pam, but I'm sure the time will come when you'll
want to visit me."
        "But Preston, I can't..."

Preston interrupted Pam.

"Are you saying you don't like your gift?"

"Yes doctor, I love the kit, but..."

"That's all I wanted to know. I'll see you later Pam."

Preston hung the phone up before Pamela could utter another word.

Sarah paced back and forth in her home. The doorbell rang, and she crouched to look out of her window. A young Hispanic woman stood outside her door.

"Tricia, come in," she said, closing the door behind her guest.

"You must really have an emergency to offer me so much money to watch Dillon."

Sarah ran through the house looking for an envelope.

"It's just for a couple of days. Here's one hundred dollars."

"She passed Tricia the money, along with a book bag filled with clothing.

"Take twenty dollars out to pay for his food, and you can keep the rest," said Sarah.

"Where are you going, anyway?"

"I really can't say. I just need you to take care of Dillon while I'm gone. OK?"

"No problem," she replied.

Sarah pushed the photocopies in the envelope, along with a note. She addressed the letter to Pamela, and gave them to her babysitter.

"I need you to mail this as soon as you can. It's important."

"Like I said, no problem," Tricia replied.

"You don't even have a stamp on here."

"I didn't have time to get any. Just get one for me."

Sarah nudged Tricia out of her home and kissed little Dillon on the head. She was nearly in tears, as the two entered the car. Slamming the door behind them, Sarah began to pack her own items.

'I forgot to pack Dillon's diapers,' Sarah thought. She heard a car pull in front of her home. The doorbell rang. Grabbing a package with her son's diapers, Sarah quickly opened the door.

"Hello Sarah," said Preston, forcing his way into her home.

Sarah tried to press her way past the doctor, but he was too strong. Before she could muster a mere whimper, Preston was behind her with a scalpel placed firmly against her neck.

"Where are my pictures?" he asked.

"I don't know what you're talking about, doctor. Please don't hurt me."

Preston pushed the blade into Sarah's skin.

"You know damn well what pictures I'm talking about. Where are my pictures?"

"There on top of the television. You can have them."

Ushering Pam toward the floor model television, the doctor maintained his tight grip around Sarah's neck. He pushed the miscellaneous papers around, until he came upon his possessions.

"Where are the copies, Sarah?"

"I don't know. Everything's there, right on the TV."

"I'll give you one more chance to tell me where the copies of my pictures are," said Preston.

"I told you, Doctor Percival. I don't know where they are," Sarah shouted.

"Well, you're out of chances."

Sarah screamed and squirmed within Preston's grasp.

He pushed the blade in deeper.

"Grab that pen and write what I tell you to write."

Following the doctor's orders, Sarah recorded Preston's statement.

"Whoever finds this letter, tell my son I love him. I don't deserve to live anymore. I don't want to live anymore. There's no need to shed any tears for me. Goodbye."

Realizing what was going on, Sarah cried while she wrote the letter. She bit Preston's arm, taking a small chunk of flesh beneath his shirt. Finally able to brake free of Preston's grip, Sarah grabbed the telephone and dashed into the bathroom. She was able to dial 91 before Preston kicked in the door. She couldn't press the last digit. Knocking Sarah into the bathtub, Doctor Percival pressed his palm against her face. With her head held upright, Preston made one precise cut across Sarah's throat. Blood barely streamed out of the wound, but her life flowed away from her. He took a knife from the kitchen and placed the blade softly into the deadly scalpel inflicted cut. It was then that the wound began to flow. Moving the body in an unsuspicious position, Preston placed the knife in Sarah's hands. The doctor made one last search for the copies, before removing his surgical gloves. He looked through the window for potential witnesses. Not one person was in the vicinity, so Preston left the home and drove away.

Preston was enthused about the elimination of the potential disruption to his relationship with Pam. He still had concerns about location of the remaining copies of his photos, but assumed Sarah had given him the most important ones. He placed one of the pictures of Pam on the front of his dashboard, tenderly touching it with his index finger. Arriving at his office, Preston searched the internet for the addresses of the women Pamela described through hypnosis. He found the listed address of Sierra Dimaano, and immediately drove there. In the passenger seat was the sculpting kit, packed just as it was in the store.

Chapter 7

Pam had been having a great deal of trouble sleeping. Restless nights had been disrupting her sleep for weeks, until she finally began taking the medicine Preston gave her. Placing two white pills in her mouth and chasing them with a Dixie cup full of water, Pam made an attempt to fall asleep once again. She put on a long polyester shirt, red in color with a flower stenciled on the front. Laying her head against the pillow, the artist fell sound asleep. Around three o'clock in the morning, Pam found herself laying in the back yard. A passing police siren woke her from her rest. Disoriented, Pam looked around in all directions. She had no idea how she arrived in the back yard. She was even more confused about her clothing. Instead of the shiny red shirt she wore to bed, Pam donned one of her husband's work shirts. She had never sleep walked before, and the thought she had done such a thing puzzled her. Pamela sprinted through the unlocked door, deciding not to tell anyone about the incident.

While driving, Preston recalled his involvement with Sierra. It was shortly after his lone date with Jenna, when she did not return his call. Sierra was a beautiful young woman, and Preston found her difficult to resist. Though he had always been infatuated with Jenna, she never showed him affection. There were neither friendly hugs given, nor the holding of hands. Sierra was different. She walked around the medical college turning all the heads with her provocative outfits. Though there were two women, Sierra and Tania, dressed in the sexy attire. Sierra was the one who caught Preston's eyes. His attraction to dark hair was evident in his pursuit of her.

He recalled the way she smiled at him. She had a "take me right now" kind of look on her face. He believed no one would know if he fooled around with her. He didn't care, as long as his beautiful "girlfriend" Jenna didn't find out. Sierra approached him, he assumed, because of his good looks. All the male medical students were jealous of Preston, while the female students despised her for her exhibitions.

"Hey doctor, I think I need a checkup" she said.

"I'm not a doctor, yet," Preston replied.

"I know, but I just want to help you get through school."

"How can you help me?" he asked.

"I can teach you things about the human body you won't learn in school." She stroked his chest, while Steve stood in amazement next to Preston.

"So what are you doing later?" Sierra asked.

"My buddy Steve and I are hanging out tonight. We'll probably shoot pool or something. After the all the test we've been taking, we need some relaxation."

"My girl Tania is gonna be with me tonight. Do you mind if we meet you up there?"

"Hell no," Preston shouted. "The more, the merrier. She looks kinda young, though"

"No, she's just a year younger than me."

At the pool hall, Sierra constantly held one to Preston's arm. He knew something was suspicious about her, from the looks she exchanged with Tania, to the notes she scribbled when Preston's back was turned. He eased his cautious demeanor when Sierra whispered in her ear.

"I know a place where we can be alone. Do you want to go with me?"

"Sure, we can go right now."

She drove him to an empty drive in.

"I want you to take your clothes off," she said.

As Preston complied, Sierra slowly unbuttoned her shirt. Preston was excited, and rushed to remove his clothing.

"There's not much room in here. Why don't you change outside?" she asked.

Preston gave no verbal response. He jumped out of the car, tossing his clothing through the open car door and into the back seat. When he was naked, after removing his tight white underwear, he looked in anticipation to Sierra. The car doors had been closed, the windows were rolled up, and Sierra had locked the doors.

"What are you doing," Preston asked?

He banged his hand against the window. Sierra blew him a kiss, as she buttoned her shirt back up. Preston realized it was part of a game, and he had just been played. The seductive vixen had his clothes inside the car, as the embarrassed medical student attempted to cover his exposed body with his hands. Sierra laughed at him, and Preston's anger rose. She called the police on her mobile phone.

"Say cheese," said Sierra.

A flash of light came from inside the Volvo, and Sierra drove away with his underwear dragging from the car's underbody.

Preston chased the car more than five blocks before he tired out. Perspiration flowed down his chest, and he stopped, resting his hands on his knees. It wasn't long before the police had the barely dressed man in handcuffs for his lack of clothing.

When Jenna found out about Preston's escapades, she avoided him. When he complimented her on her outfits, she completely changed her style. When he mentioned how he loved her long, dark hair, she cut it short and dyed it blonde. These changes infuriated Preston, though his feelings for Jenna transcended his negativity.

Jenna refused to let Preston take her picture, and became disgusted with his presence. Preston remembered the way she began to look at him, as he seemed no different than the landscape to her. He knew she had found out about the Sierra incident, but had no knowledge of how she obtained that information. It had to be Sierra, or one of her friends.

"Kill two birds with one stone," he mumbled, as he drove toward his destination. "Or three," said Preston.

Utilizing the immaculate kit Preston purchased for her Pam worked on her clay bust. The faceless sculpture had begun to take form. The tranquil eyes exhibited a profound calmness in the sculpture. Pam had moved to finish the creases in her lips, when exhaustion set in. Only the noise created by the thunderstorm outside kept Pam from falling victim to her pillow. The rigorous crafting had taken Pamela's strength away and she became incredibly weary. She took two more pills, and changed into a light blue gown. Sleep soon followed her work, and Pam began to dream. Through the dream, she observed a woman enjoying a warm shower. There were noises heard down the stairs. Not until after she applied a cold cream facial mask, did the woman pay any attention to the rumbling. She wrapped a Terri cloth towel abound her hair, and her crème robe around her still dripping body and slowly walked toward the door. There was a shadowy figure crawling beneath the slightly open window, yet the woman was unaware of it.

Through her dream, Pam screamed to warn the woman of the stranger's presence. Pamela tossed and turned in the bed in response to the nightmare. There was no sign the woman could hear her scream. The dark figure reached its gloved fingers through the small opening of the window, raising it up with a squealing noise.

"Look out," Pam screamed.

For a moment, the woman looked as if she might have heard Pam's warning, but she hunched her shoulders and continued her search. A quick survey of her property seemed to indicate all was clear. The door was still locked, and the windows were shut. Momentarily letting her guard down, the woman began to watch herself in the mirror, turning in all directions to observe her figure through the damp bathrobe. In the mirror, she saw the reflection of the shadow approaching her from behind and pounced upon her. As the sound of her scream came from deep within her, it never reached her mouth. Before she had a chance, the figure wrapped its forearm around her neck.

"Stop, let her go," Pam shouted from her dream world. A ray of light reflected on a small object within the man's grasp. When it moved across the woman's throat, a loud shriek was heard. It wasn't until the killer had the opportunity to see her face, did the killer identify the victim. He looked at his victim, turning her over. A muffled voice came from the figure, as he clutched the lifeless face of his victim.

"Damn, wrong girl."

He saw the woman's brown leather phonebook resting on the top of a small bookshelf. Flipping through the book, the shadow ripped out a few pages, and moved toward the door. As he prepared to exit the home, the killer saw the woman begin to move. He slowly walked back to her.

"Stop it," Pam screamed.

The dark killer once again raised the deadly object. It came down with full force, abruptly waking Pam from her sleep. She jumped up, panting and sweating. Wiping the sweat away Pam found relief in the fact the incident was within a nightmare. She trembled when she saw that instead of her gown, she was dressed in her husband's black coveralls. She rolled over in her bed, only to see the sculpture she created next to the bed. The feminine sculpture's head turned and stared at Pam. Its eyes were that of a living person, not simply a piece of clay. The bust suddenly opened its mouth and screamed. The scream was so loud and piercing, Pam could feel it down her spine. Face to face, they stared at each other, while the sculpture continued to scream. Pam saw a long gash along the neck of the bust.

She kicked the piece until it rolled under the bed. Pam looked underneath the bed, anticipating some terrible event. The sculpture lay on the side of its head. There was a disturbing silence. Pam pulled the piece out by its base, and rolled it over. The face had been smeared to the point its characteristics had disappeared.

Pam lay back in bed, trying to figure out what had taken place moments earlier. Unable to sleep, she turned on her 27 inch television. The news was on, and the top story was a murder which occurred on the south side of town. The newscaster portrayed the killing as a burglary gone wrong, and described the perpetrator as "a man dressed in dark clothing who killed a woman shortly after she exited the shower." They mentioned the fact her throat had been slashed. Pam was shocked, sitting with her mouth open while the story went on.

"I can't believe this," she said.

She reached for the telephone, but there was no dial tone. The storm had knocked the line down. The bad weather intensified, and large booms of thunder kept Pam on edge. Lightning sliced across the black skies, illuminating the ominous trees surrounding her house. She wished Duncan was home. Just his availability alone would have given Pam a sense of comfort on such a troubling night. Duncan, however, was not expected to be back until around noon the following day.

Pam faintly heard footsteps at the front door. She tried the telephone once again, but the line remained dead. Grabbing a broomstick, Pam stood on the side of the door. She refused to become an unaware victim, as the young woman in her nightmare had been. Clutching the handle,

Pam stood like a child prepared to hit a ball off a tee. The door knob turned, but the intruder couldn't seem to get it open. There was a loud bump against the wooden door, which frightened Pam. She dropped the broom on the carpet. Stooping to retain her weapon, Pam heard a more intense bang against the door. Just as she retrieved the broomstick, the door burst open and a man entered. Pam blindly swung as hard as she could, but the man managed to step away from the blow.

"Hold up, it's me," said the voice.

Pam scurried backward, straining her eyes to see who the stranger was. Around the open door walked Duncan, with his arms full of hunting gear.

"Duncan," screamed Pam, racing to embrace him. She wrapped her arms halfway around his thick waist and kissed him on the cheek.

"I didn't think you were coming back until tomorrow. Is everything alright?"

"No honey, something happened up there," Duncan replied.

"What happened?" asked Pam.

"Donald's dead."

"Donald's dead? What happened to him?"

"I really don't know. I guess somebody shot him. With all those new hunters up there, it's a miracle somebody else isn't dead. I just can't believe its Donald."

For some reason, Pam's mind moved toward Preston.

"Did you see Doctor Percival up there?"

"No I didn't see him up there. Why the hell would he be up there?"

"He's a hunter, too. He told me he would be up there. I was just wondering if anything happened to him."

"How would I know? I'm glad you're concerned about your doctor, while my best friend has a three inch hole through his chest."

"I was just asking, Duncan. Don't take it so personal. You know I'm concerned about Donald."

"Aren't you concerned about me?"

"Of course I'm concerned about you. I just wish you would have stayed here. None of this would have happened."

The thought of Donald's death nearly brought Duncan to tears, but he decided to head down to the basement.

"Why are you going down there," asked Pam?

"I just need a little time to get my head together."

"Duncan, I wish you would talk to me," said Pam.

"I wish I could talk to you," replied Duncan.

He slowly descended into the basement.

Duncan was in a deep sleep, as shown by his loud baritone snoring. A few cans of beer were sprawled across the floor. While Duncan soundly slept, Preston called Pamela at her home.

"Hey baby. How are you today?"

"I'm doing a little better. Things are a little crazy, but I'm hanging in there."

"I heard you had some tragedy strike your family," said Preston. "I'm sorry about your loss."

"Oh, you heard about what happened."

"Yes Pam, I heard about the incident. I don't want you to worry, because I'm here to take care of you. I'll make sure that you won't live alone."

"What are you talking about, Preston."

"Your husband, I heard he was killed up north."

"My husband...killed? Who told you that," Pam asked?

"Um...I heard about it when I was up there. I heard there was somebody shooting people up there, and your husband was killed."

"No Preston, it wasn't Duncan. Someone shot his friend Donald."

"I'm sorry Pam. I guess I got my information mixed up."

"It's alright Preston. I appreciate you asking about him."

"I just want you to be careful. If there's someone out to hurt him, I couldn't bear to see you in danger."

"I don't think I'm in any danger, Preston. Like my husband said, it's a wonder more people aren't killed up there. Did you have any trouble?"

Preston's tone changed.

"Nah Pam, I didn't have any problems at all. I hate to have to cut you off, but I have to go."

Preston hung up on Pam, disappointed to learn he had failed to kill Duncan, instead shooting his friend Donald. He knew Pamela's love for her husband, but was also aware of the friction in their relationship. Knowing their relationship was a roadblock to his own relationship with Pam, there was more work for him to do.

Pam was left confused. She had no idea what Preston was talking about, and longed for a better explanation from Duncan concerning the incident. Curiosity began to infest her mind.

As Pam moved closer to her husband, her eyes caught hold of a knife underneath the sofa. Inching closer to the cutlery, Pam saw blood drops all along the knife. Holding her hand over her mouth to contain her scream, Pam began to wonder where the blood came from. She dipped under the couch, careful not to wake her sleeping husband.

Rambling through his pockets, Pam pulled out a few dollars, a compass, and a business card. Both the money and the card were stained with blood. Through the smudges on the card, Pamela read the typed lettering. It read "Sierra Dimaano, Project Manager". She turned the card over and found some scribbling on the back of the card. She could make out the word "Payback", but the rest of the writing was illegible. A million thoughts ran through Pam's mind, and Duncan was at the center of each one.

Did Duncan have something to do with Donald's death? Where did all the blood on the knife come from? Did this have anything to do with her dream? Was the woman in her nightmare Sierra? Did Duncan kill Sierra? Did he do it to protect me?

The doorbell rang, and Pam scampered toward the window. The two officers from the hospital stood outside, with the smaller one straining to see through the drawn curtains. He caught a glimpse of Pam, who quickly moved away from the window. In a moment of panic, Pam grabbed the knife and dashed into the bathroom. Over and over again, she washed the knife. Though the blood had been removed the second the warm water hit the handle, Pam continued to scrub the knife. Once she was somewhat satisfied with her cleaning, wrapped it in newspapers and threw it into the trash bin. Duncan remained asleep, without noticing any of Pam's work.

The lieutenant began to bang on the door, while the smaller officer searched the perimeter of the home.

"Who is it?" Pam asked.

"Mrs. Fontain, you know full well who it is," screamed the officer.

"This is Lieutenant Douglas. I need you to open the door so that we can talk to Mr. Fontain."

Pam opened the door, trying to conceal the guilty expression on her face.

"What's wrong, officer? Why do you need to speak to my husband?"

"We'll explain everything to you once you tell us where your husband is located," said Lieutenant Douglas.

"He's sleeping in the basement."

Officer Davis stepped in front of the lieutenant.

"Are you going to get him, or do we need to grab him ourselves?"

"No, I'll get him," Pam replied.

She darted down the stairs, rocking Duncan from side to side until he awoke.

"What is it," asked Duncan? He wiped the drool from the corner of his mouth.

"The police are here. They want to talk to you."

"Did they say what they wanted?" Duncan asked.

"No, they wouldn't tell me anything."

Duncan fumbled with his socks, before putting on his steel toed work boots.

"Maybe they found the person who shot Donald."

While Duncan was walking up the stairs leading to the first floor, Officer Davis was planted on the middle step. He watched the entire interaction between the two. Duncan rubbed his eyes, as he sluggishly maneuvered his way into the living room. He smiled at the lieutenant, offering a handshake. The steel faced officer declined.

"So, did you find out anything about the hunter who shot Donald?"

"Well, Mr. Fontain, it's a little more complicated than that."

Officer Davis moved behind Duncan.

"You have the right to remain silent. Anything you say can and will be used against you in a court of law."

Duncan's mouth dropped.

"What is this? You're arresting me?"

The lieutenant continued.

"You have a right to speak to an attorney, and have an attorney present during any questioning. If you cannot afford a lawyer, one will be provided for you at government expense. Do you understand these rights?"

Duncan looked bewildered at Pam, who had both of her hands covering her mouth.

"Yeah, but I..."

Before Duncan was able to finish his statement, Officer Davis had grabbed his arm. Duncan reflexes caused him to pull away, until the lieutenant reached for his firearm.

"You don't want to do that, big fella," said Lieutenant Douglass.

Duncan allowed the small officer to place him in handcuffs.

"What did I do wrong?" he asked.

"You're being placed under arrest for the death of Donald Lanier. We have a sworn statement from a witness who says they saw you kill him up north."

"They said what? I didn't kill Donald. That was my best friend. Pam, tell them I didn't kill Donald."

Lieutenant Douglas escorted him out. Before leaving their home, he glared at Duncan.

"Mr. Fontain, I'm going to advise you to remain silent. I'm not going to tell you again."

"Pam, say something," Duncan screamed. "Pam!"

She ran toward Duncan, but was restrained by Officer Davis.

"He didn't do it. I know my husband."

The lieutenant rushed him into the squad car, while Pam pushed and shoved to get around the officer. Once the door shut Duncan within the vehicle, Pam eased her struggle.

At the police station, Duncan was fingerprinted, searched, and his mug shots were taken. He sat on a stiff wooden bench, unpleasantly set two feet off the concrete. After a prolonged period of time waiting for someone to provide information to him concerning his arrest, Duncan was approached by Lieutenant Douglas and an unfamiliar officer. The officer guided Duncan into a dark room lighted by a single 30 watt bulb. He was sat down at a senselessly scratched wood table. There were names, profane statements, and gang related symbols etched into the table. Lieutenant Douglas sat next to Duncan in a chair turned backward.

"Here we are, Mr. Fontain. I'm going to make this as efficient as possible. Tell me what happened up north with you and Mr. Lanier."

Duncan began to speak, but was interrupted by the lieutenant.

"Let me inform you, Duncan. I'm a human lie detector. I've been in this business over twenty five years, and I'll read you like an open book, so you better not lie to me."

Duncan turned to Lieutenant Douglas, looking him square in the eyes.

"I don't have any reason to lie," said Duncan. "Donald and I went up to Wisconsin to hunt some deer. When we spotted one about a mile from the cabin, I ran it toward him. Donald shot his gun, and the next thing I know, he was laying on the ground with a hole in his chest."

"So you have no idea who shot him?" the lieutenant asked.

"No, I don't know who shot him. If I did, I would have shot them back."

Lieutenant Douglas gazed at Duncan, trying to detect any movement in his eyes that would give indication of his falsehood. Duncan's eyes were set on him, as he stood unflinching at the scrutiny placed upon him. The lieutenant continued to stare, aggressively chewing on the cap of his Bic pen. After jotting down a few notes, he vaulted from his chair. Snatching his folder from the table, he trudged around Duncan, patting him on the shoulder.

After her first confusing attempt at the sculpture and the disruptive incidents that followed, Pam worked diligently on another bust. She was aware of the necessity to finish her project. It would take far more money than they possessed to post Duncan's bond. The medical bills had added up astronomically, and despite Duncan's double shifts, there was little in their savings account. Her failure to complete the first sculpture potentially cost them thousands of dollars. This led to her second attempt.

Out of a wood grained chest, Pam extracted her clays. The standard grayish clay was in one section of the chest, while the special brownish clay lay in another section.

She spent a few hours molding the shape of the bust, before focusing on the features. Experimenting with a variety of unique texture adding tools, Pam began to visualize the fruits of her labor. She fought through her physical and mental exhaustion, as well as the fear of another nightmare, approaching the completion of her sculpture. As the sun set and the night exposed itself, Pam's hands ached. She smiled at the completed sculpture. The beauty of the woman Pam created was immeasurable. Her exotic eyes looked off into a distance, while her hair twisted and tangled in a natural fashion. The bust was set on top of the dresser. Pam placed a wooden crate over the bust to prevent any nicks or scratches.

Confident about the success of her project, Pam was finally able to relax. She remained dressed in her charcoal gray sweatshirt, despite its soiled appearance from her clay work. Mired in a drained state, Pam didn't bother to change, simply lying in her bed. Although she tried to resist, Pam's body could no longer be deprived of rest. Before she could catch herself, Pam fell into a deep sleep and crashed into another dream.

In this dream, a youthful looking black woman was exercising on a treadmill. She wore a jet black spandex suit with a bright red stripe running along its side. As the pace of her trot increased, her awareness of the situation diminished. Soulful music blared through her Sony headphones, masking the noises just outside of her small two-bedroom home. There was the pounding of nails near the windows and doors, before a presence moved into the kitchen. Opening the top of the gas range, the pilot light was extinguished. The dark figure turned the dials on the stove to its highest setting, and gas filled the house. Thick fumes quickly filled every crevice of the living area, settling within her overworked lungs.

Within minutes, the woman became lightheaded. She stumbled off the exercise equipment, dropping to all fours. Crawling toward the door, the woman gasped for air. She reached for the door knob, pulling as hard as she could, but the door would not budge. Struggling to obtain any semblance of air, she used all of her remaining energy to crawl to the double paned window.

Pam was helpless to assist the woman. She could only watch the frightened look on her face. The woman tried to lift the window, but the long dark nail embedded from the outside prevented it from opening. She swung her hand against the window, trying to break the glass. Her strength had dwindled to the point where she was ineffective. As she slumped beneath the sill, Pam saw a ball of fire crash through the window. The woman looked upward, as a bottle flew over her head and against the wall. She watched the bottle, filled with a liquid and a flaming towel, sitting twelve feet away from her. She screamed, and there was a huge explosion. Fire shot out of every direction. The blast was so loud it shook Pam out of her dream, and placed her back into reality.

As she cleared her eyes, trying to comprehend the nightmare, there was a strong odor within the room. Pam looked around her space, and saw smoke coming from within the box on top of her dresser. The smoke caused Pam to cough. She slowly walked around the bed toward the box. Concerned about the condition of her sculpture, Pam lifted the box. Underneath the box, she found the charred remains of the bust. Moving closer, Pam hesitantly touched the bust. A small chip of the bust fell off. When she turned to get a garbage bag to place the piece into, she saw the lips of the sculpture tremble. Jumping back, Pam stared at the piece.

"Help me," said a soft voice from the piece, and then it stopped.

Pam ran to the bathroom, throwing up for more than fifteen minutes. When she peeked around the corner to observe the sculpture, it had broken in pieces next to the box.

Chapter 8

It was nearly two full days later when Tricia rediscovered Sarah's letter. Searching for a honey melon lipstick lost a week earlier, she dipped into the unorganized glove compartment in her yellow Pontiac Sunfire. The letter was partially crumpled, but the mailing address was still visible. Tricia pulled it out and set it on the passenger's seat. She drove to the check cashing store and purchased three stamps from the money left over for Dillon's food. Placing the stamp on the letter, she tossed it into the mailbox, unaware of its importance.

Pam walked to their mailbox attached to the siding on their house. There were four pieces of mail within the confines of the box. Picking through the envelopes, she set aside the three obvious bill statements. The last envelope was torn, with a grease stain near the flap. It smelled similar to the pine air freshening trees. Pam ripped the envelope open with the blade of a butter knife. She hoped it wasn't a letter from Sierra, but was eager to find out. Unfolding the wrinkled letter, she smoothed it with the palm of her hand on her wooden cutting board. Pam surveyed the page, noticing the curious traits it possessed. The letter's hurried penmanship marked the frantic nature of its author. On a single sheet of college ruled paper was a message from Sarah.

"Pam, you have to stay away from Doctor Percival. He has pictures of you everywhere and I think he's crazy. I don't want to see you hurt, so stay as far away from him as possible. P.S. Don't tell him that I wrote this letter. I've seen him upset. I don't know what would happen to me if he found out I told you."

Looking further into the envelope, she found copies of the pictures. Some where photos of her in the hospital sleeping, while other pictures hadn't been seen since high school. There were also copies of some pictures of a woman with similar characteristics to Pam. Placing her hand on her forehead, Pam dropped down to the edge of the bed. She grabbed her preferred provider booklet, and searched its contents for the direct line of Doctor Bradley. When the number was found, Pam immediately called the one person close to Preston.

"Doctor Bradley, this is Pamela Fontain."

How's it going, Pam?"

"Not too good, doctor. I got a letter from your secretary Sarah."

"A letter from Sarah? I wonder why she would send you a letter. Was it concerning her firing?"

"She was fired?"

"Yes Pam. Unfortunately she's no longer with the hospital."

"Oh, really? How long ago was that?"

"That happened recently. One of the doctor's felt we needed to go in another direction. What type of letter did she send you? I hope it wasn't anything offensive."

"Well, it wasn't just a letter. She also sent me copies of some pictures he took of me. I didn't give him permission to take my picture."

"What kind of pictures?"

"There wasn't anything provocative. They were mostly pictures of me in the hospital, but he also had some of my old high school pictures. I don't know how he got them or why he has them."

"I have no idea, Pam."

"There were pictures of another woman."

"What other woman?" asked Doctor Bradley.

"She has long brown hair and...she kind of looks like me. There are a lot of pictures of her."

"Oh, pictures of her."

"You know who I'm talking about, don't you?" asked Pam.

"I'm sorry Pamela. As much as I would like to help you, there are some things I can't disclose. I have to draw the line somewhere."

Pam screamed into the receiver.

"You have to tell me what's going on. I can't take this anymore, and if something happens to me, it'll be your fault."

Steve thought about the situation, and gave in to Pam's request.

"Alright, I'll tell you. The pictures are of a young lady named Jenna. Preston had a huge crush on her, but they never really got together. When she died a few years later, he had trouble dealing with it."

"Oh my God," said Pam. "How did she die?"

"No one knows how she died, but they ruled it a suicide. I still don't think he's over her. I'm not sure why he has your pictures, but you do favor her. Maybe he's interested in you."

"I don't want to deal with him anymore."

"Didn't you say that you received a letter from Sarah? What did it say?"

"She told me to leave Doctor Percival alone. It sounded like she was afraid of him. That's why I called you. You two work together, so I thought you could tell me if this is something he does all the time."

"I wouldn't say this is something he does all the time, but it doesn't surprise me."

"Is there anything you can do? Can't you talk to him?"

"I can try, but Preston is pretty stubborn."

"Doctor, you have to talk to him. I can't deal with this. I'm having nightmares, seeing things, talking to myself. He's probably trying to drive me crazy. Maybe I'm already crazy."

"Pam, you're not crazy. If Preston told you that, he's lying. Do you remember when I told you that you had some swelling around the limbic area?"

"Yes, I remember you saying something like that."

"Well, I probably should have gone into greater detail about the situation. The limbic system is the area that regulates emotion. It is commonly referred to as the 'lizard brain' because of its primitive nature. It lies along the margin of the cerebral cortex and includes the amyglada, hippocampus, and other components which interact with the thalamus and hypothalamus and govern aggressive behavior. It is involved with skills such as memory, language, motivation and drive. When that region is damaged, it can affect decision making and problem solving, negative emotions, and social isolation. Malfunctions in the system can lead to deranged behavior. Especially if you're having nightmares,"

"I've been having nightmares like you wouldn't believe."

"If you didn't remember your nightmare, I would say you're experiencing Sleep Terror Disorder. Since you do remember them, there could be another diagnosis. It could be a sign of a nightmare disorder. That's a condition where you relive a traumatic event in your life over and over again through a nightmare. That's probably why you're so tired. From what I know of you, you don't fit the profile of a killer. I believe someone is playing with your head. I don't know if that person is Preston or not, but I wouldn't trust Doctor Percival if I were you."

"Why shouldn't I trust him?" asked Pam.

"He may be my friend, but Preston has a lot of issues. I probably should have turned him in a while ago, but he has a lot of pull. People end up fired, reassigned, or blackballed when they come up against Preston. He's probably had ten to fifteen sexual harassment accusations since he's been here."

"So why does he still have a job?" she asked.

"Because he's damn good," said Doctor Bradley. "If you give him a scalpel, he's like an artist. I've never seen anyone like him. Don't get me wrong. I'm pretty good myself, but in my twelve years as a surgeon, I've never seen anyone work like him. We operated on you together, with the help of Doctor Hammonds. Still, I have no idea why he didn't inform you of all the facts. Maybe he wanted you to think you were going crazy."

"So what is wrong with me, doctor? What does this limbic stuff have to do with these dreams and sleepwalking?"

Pamela listened intensely.

"The limbic system is called the 'primate state' for a reason. It gets us ready to fight or run when something threatens us. It is very powerful and not rational. Memory also has a lot to do with it. For instance, when you were involved in your car accident, the emotional component of that memory is stored in the limbic system. The emotions of a positive memory, such as your wedding anniversary, are also stored in that region. As far as your sleep problems, it's all associated with the limbic system. An unhealthy sleep pattern is often a problem connected to limbic abnormalities. There have even been rare cases where people have committed crimes they didn't remember."

"I couldn't have killed anyone. I would never hurt another human being."

"I'm not saying you did, Pamela."

"Then why do I remember the murders?" she asked.

"There is a thing called false memory," answered Doctor Bradley.

"What does that mean?"

"A false memory is when the brain consolidates pieces of memory that are scattered through the brain and assembles them as if they were from one true event. Often, part of the memory is true, while the other comes from suggestion. When an individual is under emotional stress, they tend to be more sensitive to this. Sometimes a treatment such as hypnosis can corrupt memories instead of retrieving them."

"Hypnosis ... that asshole. Did you know that he tried to hypnotize me last week? He told me it would help me remember."

"It can help you to remember in many cases. Hopefully, he's not doing it for the wrong reasons."

"I didn't even think I could be hypnotized."

"Medical hypnosis is about ideas influencing responses. How did he do it?"

"He told me to think of peaceful places, count from one to one hundred, and other stuff like that."

"Yeah Pam, he was just trying to relax you."

"Why would he do that?"

"Relaxing the body while creating a state of mental awareness can makes it easy to assimilate therapeutic suggestions."

"How do you know so much about psychology?"

"Do you think Preston's the only neurosurgeon that has a degree in psychology? We both attended the same medical school and we both were at the top in our class. He just has more natural ability, while I had to work like hell to get to where I am. He is my friend, but he's not the friend I used to know. He's really changed. Ever since he took those martial arts classes, he's been different."

"What do you mean by different?" asked Pam.

"He's gotten really vain since he started working out. It's not just the vanity thing. It's his anger. He's always looking for a fight. I remember the time some guys broke into his house. It was about two weeks after he bought it. He spent all this money on the electronics and the furniture he'd always wanted. They came in when Preston was asleep and woke him up by pistol whipping him. They tied him up with his own stethoscope, and made him watch his belongings being stolen.

They took everything, except the stuff he hid in the attic. It drove him crazy when the police couldn't find the thieves. After the insurance company replaced the stolen items, Preston took those martial arts classes. He put all these locks on the doors and steel bars on the windows."

"I don't blame him for wanting to keep the robbers out," said Pam.

"He didn't do it to keep the robbers out. He wanted to lock them in."

"Why would he do that?"

"Preston came up with a plan. He used the big screen plasma television he bought as bait. When the same two thieves saw that the lights were turned off, no cars were in the driveway, and the curtains were open, they broke into the house. The robbers entered through the same back window as before. Preston left the on the window unlocked purposely. While they were moving the television toward the back door, Preston hit them on the back of their legs with a baseball bat. He locked the doors so they couldn't escape, and beat the two men for more than twenty minutes before he called the police. You should hear the way he describes it, talking about the sound of their broken bones and all this nonsense. I guess he thinks he's a hero, but I think he's crazy. I never knew he had a dark side like that."

"So you understand why I want you to tell him to stop calling me. If he doesn't, I'm going to have to tell my husband. He's already suspicious of him."

"Alright Pam, I'll talk to him tonight after work. We'll see what happens."

After an extremely long day at the hospital, Doctor Bradley approached Preston.

"Man, this was one heck of a day."

"You're telling me," said Preston. He removed his medical attire as he headed to his office.

"Preston, I need to talk to you," screamed Steve as he jogged behind his coworker.

"I can't do it, man. I'm done for the day," said Preston.

"Oh, now you're to busy to talk to me, huh?"

"Hell yeah, man."

Preston put his hand on Steve's shoulder.

"Look man, there are three types of celebrities; entertainers, lawyers, and surgeons. I'm like the freakin rock star of surgery. They make movies about people like me."

Steve laughed, anticipating a laugh from Preston. Doctor Percival merely gave a courteous smile, unable to figure out what the joke was. They left the facility and heading toward the parking structure.

"What are you talking about?"

"Whatever you want me to do, I can't do it. I'm done for the day."

"Preston, this ain't about work. It's about your personal life."

"What about my personal life?"

"It's about Pamela Fontain."

Preston stopped in front of the entrance to the parking structure and glared at Steve.

"What about Pamela Fontain?"

"Look man, I don't want to get into your business, but you should leave Mrs. Fontain alone. She's had a lot of difficulty with her recovery, and

I don't think playing with her head is going to help her at all."

"What the hell are you talking about, Steve?"

"Come on Preston, you know what I'm talking about," said Dr. Bradley. "You're using all that psycho bull crap to get into her pants. Don't you have enough women? Do you really have to start sleeping with our patients?"

Preston's eyes blazed through Dr. Bradley.

"Are you jealous or something?" asked Preston.

"I don't have anything to be jealous about. I'm just looking out for our patients," Steve replied.

"First of all they're not our patients, they're my patients. They don't come to see you. They come to see me. They only come to see you when I'm not available. Secondly, what gives you the right to question who I choose to date?" he asked.

"What gives you the right to use your profession to manipulate a patient?" asked Steve. "The patients put their trust in us, and when you betray that trust, you make it hard for all of us to do our jobs."

"You weren't saying that when I was using my profession to help you find a date, now were you?"

"What happened when we were young doesn't matter now. What matters is how you're becoming a disgrace to the profession with your actions. You're a grown man. Act like one. You can't do that to people."

Preston paused for a moment, silently processing Steve's words.

"I guess you're right, Steve. I guess I got a little carried away, buddy," said Preston.

They continued to walk down the street. Preston placed his arm around Steve's shoulder.

"Do you want to go get a drink?" Preston asked.

"Have you ever known me to turn down a drink, especially when you're buying? Where do you want to go?"

"There's a bar right across the street," said Preston pointing to the dimly lit bar. They entered the bar and had a few drinks.

"So how has things been going in your love life?" Steve asked.

"I'm still looking for that Mrs. Right, but at least I got a couple of Mrs. Right Nows."
The two men laughed.

"You still haven't found true love? Preston Percival, America's most eligible bachelor spends another lonely night at home watching ER."
"I said I haven't found another true love, I didn't say I was lonely," replied Preston.

"I always thought I would be the one who slept alone. I would have never guessed I would be married to a beautiful wife, and you would still be looking for one."
Irritated, Preston once again glared at Steve.

"Maybe I'm just a little pickier than you. I don't have to settle on the first decent looking woman who takes interest in me. I can afford to wait."

"You need to stop pretending. You're looking for Jenna and Jenna's not here anymore. I don't care how much Mrs. Fontain looks like Jenna. She's not Jenna. Let her rest in peace and take a chance with someone else."
Preston turned away from Steve's stool.

"Look man, you don't know what it's like to lose your one true love."

"I'm sure I don't, but do you know what its like to find love again? I mean real love. You'll never know until you step out and commit to something more than a one night stand. I would have never met my wife if I kept living in the past."

"Don't try to psychoanalyze me. You can't begin to understand how much I loved Jenna. It's not like you and Janet with your superficial fasad of a relationship. We were supposed to be together forever," said Preston.

"I'm so tired of you saying that you and Jenna were together. You guys didn't even really date. One date is not considered dating. I think you're losing your mind."

Preston jumped off his stool and stood next to Steve. The look on his face was more intense than any he'd ever witnessed.

"We did date, and don't ever badmouth Jenna again."

The grip on the beer Preston held in his hand was magnified until his hands became pale from the loss of circulation.

"Calm down man," said Steve. I'm not badmouthing your situation with Jenna. I'm just saying she wasn't the only fish in the sea. She's not even as holesum as you tried to make her out to be. Remember that incident in the locker room?"

"She didn't ask for that. Those guys just forced her. She wasn't that type of girl," said Preston.

"Look man, she was like the rest of the cheerleaders. She didn't even say anything until the word got around."

Preston moved face to face with Steve, leaning over in front of his stool.

"If you talk about her one more time, I'll break your freakin jaw."

The bartender grabbed a baseball bat from behind the bar and walked over to the patrons.

"You fellas are going to have to keep it down. This ain't that type of establishment. If you want to fight, you need to take it across the street.

"I'm sorry sir," said Steve. "We just got a little carried away. It won't happen again."

Preston sat back on his stool. His mood swung between anger and sadness as he fought back his tears. He rested his forearms on the top of the bar.

"Look man, I'm sorry," said Steve. "I know how you like to hold grudges, but I'm just trying to be a friend.

"Whatever friend," Preston replied.

Steve scooted his stool closer to Preston.

"All I was saying is that there are a lot of good women out there besides Jenna."

"Like the ones we dealt with in medical school?" asked Preston.

"Look Preston, you weren't the only one who got played by those chicks. The one I went out with had me chasing her car in my boxers in the middle of winter."

"Let me guess, she took your clothes."

"How did you know?"

"The girl I was with did the same to me. She took everything, except for the boxers. I don't know why we hadn't talked about this until now. I thought you said she annoyed you, so you dumped her?"

"She did annoy me, and in a way I guess I did dump her."

"Man, you are full of it. You didn't say anything about her playing you."

"Neither did you. Do you really think I wanted you to know that story?"

"You think your situation was bad? At least you didn't get arrested. They picked me up for indecent exposure. It cost my family a lot of money to make those charges disappear. They almost ruined my career. Worst of all, somebody told Jenna about it. Someday I'm gonna find out who told her and make them pay.

After three or four beers and a fairly entertaining night, the men left the bar. They walked down the pedestrian void street. Once again, Dr. Percival's arm was wrapped around his friend's shoulder. They laughed at their discussion their past experiences. Preston stumbled around the sidewalk nearly dragging Steve down with him.

As the two came to the curb, Preston's grip tightened around Steve's neck.

"What are doing, man?"

Preston pulled Steve's ear next to his face. The disturbing expression returned to his face. His grip was incredibly strong. Steve struggled to wedge his fingers in between his friend's hand, while Preston whispered in his ear.

"Do you think I forgot what you said about Jenna? I told you I wouldn't let anybody badmouth Jenna, didn't I?"

"What the hell are you talking about?" asked Steve.

"Now you want to break me and Pam up? You told her not to talk to me anymore, didn't you? You've known me long enough to know I remember everything, don't you."

Steve continued to wrestle with Preston.

"Break you up? You're living in a dream world, man."

"Shut up. You know I always do what I say I'm gonna do, right? Well I've carried your ass long enough. I helped you through high school, medical school, through licensing, and through your most difficult operations. Now you want to mess up my relationship? It's time to cut the umbilical cord, baby."

"What are you doing," Steve screamed. Through Preston's comments, he scanned the street. From a block away Preston spotted a billboard on the side of a large city bus. The bus turned the corner and headed down the street in front of the men. The headlights became brighter as the vehicle moved closer. A devious smile came across his face. As rampaging bus drew near, Preston pushed Steve in front of it.

"Steve, no...," he shouted. Steve slid to the ground, failing in his attempt to bring a halt to his momentum.

Preston covered his mouth, pretending to be in shock as the bus smashed into his companion. It sent his broken body hundreds of feet through the air, and into a street light. With a horrifying thump, Steve dropped to the pavement.

"No, man, no...," he said.
Preston dropped to his knees, crying as if it were his slain brother. A few citizens ran out of the bar, while the bus came to a screeching halt half a block away from its initial impact. Grabbing his cell phone, Preston called the hospital.

"Hello, this is Doctor Percival. We need an ambulance out here immediately. Doctor Bradley's been hit by a bus."

"Where are you, Doctor?" asked the dispatcher.

"We're about two blocks away from the hospital. I'm right in front of the bar."

"An ambulance will be there in a second, Doctor."

Preston ran down to the scene of the accident. Steve's torso was severely twisted, yet his left eye turned toward Preston. As the crowd gathered, Preston crouched over the body. Steve's eye screamed for justice to be inflicted on his betrayer, but his body failed to cooperate. While he was dying, Preston gave him a quick wink and walked away.

"He didn't make it," he said to the crowd. The ambulance arrived, but all the crew was able to do was transport the majority of Steve's body back to the hospital.

Chapter 9

Pam was distraught about the secrets she was forced to hold in. She decided to turn to her professor for the guidance necessary to finish her project and regain her sanity. From the sanctity of her bedroom, Pam called the professor.

"Hello Professor Wembly, how are you?"

"I'm doing well, Pamela. What gives me the pleasure of your telephone call?"

"I'm calling you because some strange stuff his happening with my sculptures. I hope you don't think I'm going crazy, like my husband does."

"No, tell me about it," said Professor Wembly.

"Well, it's like this. Lately I've been working on those pieces you asked me to do, and when I finish them something happens."

"Something like what?" asked Professor Wembly.

"I don't know how to put it. I guess I'll just say it. The sculptures seem to come alive. I don't know how or why, but I see them come to life. After that, I see them die."

"You see what?"

"I see the sculptures live and die, but that's not the scariest part. After the sculptures die, people die. It's like there's a connection between the two."

"I can give you the number of my psychiatrist, Pamela. He's quite good."

"I'm serious, Professor. With all due respect, I think I've had enough psychology to last me a lifetime. I just don't want to see another person die."

"Now that you mention it, I've heard someone talk about something like that recently. Now where did I hear that before?" Professor Wembly removed his eyeglasses, trapping the edge of them between his teeth. "Oh no, I hope it's not true. It couldn't be."

"What couldn't be true," asked Pam.

"Do you remember the old man that bought the piece you made?"

"Of course I remember," she answered. "Wasn't he was one of the Adam's?"

"He died a couple of weeks ago."

"Oh my goodness, Walter. How did he die?"

"He had a heart attack. His wife, or his mistress, or his 'whatever' said he saw the bust come to life. He died with his mouth and his eyes wide open from the shock. They're still treating her at the mental institute. At the time, I didn't think too much about it. As time passed, I thought about that clay you were talking about."

"Do you mean the special clay I got from New Orleans?"

"That's just what I'm talking about. You have to stop using that clay. You can't fool around with that voodoo. It's just not right."

"I'm not a bad person, professor. You know I don't do voodoo. I just used the clay," said Pam.

"If you use it, then you are participating in it. If you participate in it, strange things are bound to happen."

"You think it's my fault these people died, don't you?"

"No Pam, I don't. I just don't want to see anything happen to you. If an old man can survive two wars and live to see ninety, but die from a heart attack while watching a sculpture, something's not right."

"How do you expect me to do the same quality of work if I don't use the techniques that gave me the opportunity in the first place?"

"Pamela, some people say it's all about the art. I think its all about the artist. What good is the piece that is created without the hands of the creator? You can't compromise for the sake of a technique, Pamela."

"But we need the money," Pam screamed.

"Don't worry about the money. The offer is going to stay on the table. That's one thing you should have already known about me. I don't break the promises I make to my students. It's best not to become too focused on the money. When artists do that, they lose touch with the reason they became involved in the first place. I know it wasn't just to make money and practice that voodoo mumbo jumbo."

"I thought you didn't believe in voodoo," said Pam. "Didn't you call it nonsense?" Professor Wembly sighed.

"My dear, I'm not here to argue with you. I just wish you could believe in your creativity like I do. There is no need for you to dabble in this foolishness. You have to promise me you will stop this right now."

"I'm sorry professor. I just can't promise that right now. It's not just about the money. There are so many questions I need answered, and this is the only way I know to find them."

"I truly believe something bad is going to happen to you if you continue, Pamela," said Professor Wembly.

"What if this is just something I'm supposed to do? What if I'm supposed to keep these people from dying? Why does it have to be something bad? Maybe it's a gift I was born with."

Moments passed without teacher or student making a single comment to one another. Each reflected from the other's point of view. Pam took a deep breath.

"This will be the last time I use the clay, professor. I can promise you that."

"Promises, Promises. What if this turns into more than a bad dream this time, Pamela?" Silence returned its prominence, while Pam thought.

"I'm sorry Pamela," said Professor Wembly. "I regret the fact you were forced to listen to the ramblings of an old man."

"It's alright, professor. I respect you enough to listen to your concern for my safety. I hope you understand that I have to make the best decision for my husband and myself."
"I pray it's the right decision," said Professor Wembly. "Goodbye Pamela."

Working on her third bust, Pam thought about the concerned advice from Professor Wembly. She was aware of the possibility this sculpture could have the same disturbing effect. Pam resisted using the clay, but the quality of detail created by the special voodoo clay more than compensated for her fears. After more than three hours of work, Pam rested in the bed, hesitant to even fall asleep due to the horrific nightmares she'd been experiencing. Knowing the answers to her questions about the killer and his victim lay within her dreams, Pam utilized the same process that led to her previous nightmare.

She urged herself into a tranquil mindset. With a beige mug filled with chamomile tea and a single candle flickering in the dark room, Pam began to doze off.
Her dream began as routine as many of the others she had experience. She watched a woman walking about her home in a long linen gown. Time after time, Pam attempted focusing on the face of the woman, but was unable to see her due to the homes darkness and the woman never showing her face. In this dream, the young lady seemed to be looking around for something. She searched the closet, but found nothing inside. She searched under the bed, the area was empty.

Throughout the home, the woman's flowing robe trailed her inquisitive person. Her silky black hair draped down her back. Walking toward the unlocked front door, she thrust it open. A large hooded figure stood in the doorway. A cold breeze swept through the entrance. The gloved shadow reached into its pocket and pulled out an object with a blade pertruding from the shaft.
Through her dream, Pam's pulse began to rise as she searched for the murder's face beneath the cloak. The robed woman took a step back, holding her hand out to signal the intruder not to come any closer. Slowly and deliberately the figure moved toward her. Suddenly, it sprang upon her, tightly gripping the weapon. Like a snapshot, Pam

was finally able to see the eyes of the attacker. They were powerful blue eyes, pulsating within the face of the killer.

"Preston," Pam screamed, shocked about her discovery.
The doctor seemed to hear her call, looking around the room. He laughed, as he turned to grab the unknown woman. Holding back the blade in his right hand, Preston reared back. As he swung his blade at the woman, Pam screamed. She was able to wake herself up before the deathblow was inflicted on the woman. Drenched, Pam hesitantly turned toward the bust. She was afraid of what she would find. Once again the sculpture was next to her bedside. This time, the sculpture looked at her, attempting to scream, but the bust was incomplete. Half of the sculpture had no characteristics. There was no mouth, and only one of the eyes was complete.

The bust moaned over and over, getting louder every moment. The noise seemed to shake the pictures on the walls. Its human-like eye stared at Pam. The artist cried, fully aware of the pain the victim in her dream was likely to be subjected to. She grabbed her rosary beads, excessively rubbing her fingers against them. Pam came to the conclusion that the woman in her dream was Sierra. The killer had murdered both of her friends, so Sierra was the next logical victim. Throwing her sheets over the head of the clay busts, Pam withdrew from the room.

It was the middle of the night, but Pamela knew she couldn't wait to warn the woman. There were already two women dead, and there would be a third if Sierra weren't notified. From her business card, she was able to look up Sierra's address. Opening the curtains, Pam stared at the pickup truck outside her home. Noticing the damage to the tires, she turned to her friend Sylvia for assistance.

Pam called Sylvia more than ten times, ending her call each moment the voicemail responded. Sylvia finally answered.

"Yeah, what is it?"

"Sylvia, this is Pam. I need your help."

"I'll do anything for you, as long as I don't have to get up."

"I need to borrow your car."

"Girl, I am not getting out of this bed. Do you know how many hours I had to work today?"

"Sylvia, I really need this. You can't imagine how important this is."

"Do you have a hot date or something?"

"Sylvia, this is serious."

"I'm sorry Pam, I was just playing. Can you get a way over here?"

"I guess I can call for a cab or something."

"If you can get over here, the car's yours. You know where I keep the spare key, right?"

"Do you still keep that key under the car?"

"It's right next to the muffler. Just bring it back before seven. I have to work tomorrow."

"I will," said Pam.

"In one piece, please."

"I told you I would bring it back. Just go back to bed."

"I'm just kidding, baby. I'll see you in the morning."

Pamela called for the cab. Within an hour she was on her way to Sylvia's home. She sat upright in the back seat of the cab, straddling the large tear in the fake leather seat. Soft Arabic music played from the driver's stereo, soothing

Pam's tense state. It symbolized the calm before her anticipated storm. The driver remained silent, as Pam casually observed him through the smudged plastic barrier. The cab moved in front of the tan duplex, stopping next to Sylvia's Chrysler. After paying the driver, she reached under the cold steel underbody of the car, grabbing the magnetic key holder in her oil streaked hand. Pam entered the car and headed toward Sierra's home.

Banging on the door, Pam called the young woman's name. Sierra looked through the peep hole, and saw a familiar looking woman. It didn't take long to determine who the visitor was. Sierra looked as if she had seen a ghost. Against her better judgment, she opened the door. Pam struggled to maintain her composure, as her adversary stood in front of her.

"Long time, no see Sierra," said Pam.

"What the hell are you doing in front of my house?"

"Oh, now you have a problem with uninvited guests?"

"I hope you're not here to argue about Duncan," said Sierra.

"Look, I don't care about what happened between you and my husband. I'm trying to save your life."

"What are you talking about?"

"I saw what happened to your friends. Well, I didn't actually see it, but I know who killed them."

"Is this some type of game or something?"

Percival killed your friends, and you're gonna be next if you don't leave the state."

"Preston Percival? Who is Preston Percival?"

"Look, I don't know if you've ever met him or not, but I know he's coming after you. Maybe you should think back to all of the men you've slept with. He's probably somewhere in your rolodex."

"I'm not going to have you come to my house and insult me."

"I'm sure you'll get over it," Pam replied.

"How do you know all of this?"

"I saw it in a dream."

"You saw it in a dream," said Sierra, sarcastically.

"So, because you had some weird dream, I'm just supposed to move to another state."

"I'm just trying to save your life."

"All you're doing is wasting my time. If you're making up this story to keep me away from Duncan, you need to quit. I decided to let you have him."

"Let me have him. Bitch, I'm just trying to help you."

"Like you helped Tania and Sheila? Did you tell them about this Preston guy? Maybe there is no Preston. Maybe you killed them. I should call the cops right now and tell them you had something to do with their deaths."

"You are the last person who should want the cops involved in this. I know you had something to do with my accident."
Pam shook her head, as she walked away.

"I knew I shouldn't have come over here."

After being unable to convince Sierra of the threat Preston posed to her, Pam decided to turn to the police. She called the extension of Lieutenant Douglas.

"Lieutenant Douglas speaking," he answered.

"Hello lieutenant. This is Pamela Fontain."

"Yes, Mrs. Fontain, what can I do for you?"

"You know about all of the murders that have been going on lately?"

"Of course I do. Is there something you want to tell me about them?"
The lieutenant seemed to be prodding for more information.

"There is something, but you have to promise me you won't think this is a joke."

"Look Pam, I don't do jokes. Go ahead and tell me what's on your mind. People are dying everyday and I don't have a lot of time to chit chat."

"I know who killed those women," said Pam.

"You know what?"

"The women that have died here recently, I know who killed them."

"Who is it, Pam," said Lieutenant Douglas, reaching for his pen and pad of paper.

"His name is Preston Percival."

"Doctor Percival? Does this have anything to do with us arresting your husband? I hope you're not going to try and pin that hunter's death on Doctor Percival, because it ain't gonna happen."

"Sir, I know my husband couldn't kill a man. It's not in his nature. This isn't even about him. It's about Preston Percival killing those women.

"How did you come to this revelation?" asked the Lieutenant.

"Do you promise to take me seriously?"

"Look Pamela, I don't have time for games. Go ahead and tell me what you know."
Pam composed herself and responded to the lieutenant's request.

"I've been having dreams about the deaths of those women, and I saw that Doctor Percival killed them. I saw it before it really happened. Now there's another woman that's going to die if you don't do something to stop him."
There was a long period of silence, along with some huffing and puffing by the lieutenant.

"So this is all about some dream you had," said Lieutenant Douglas, smugly.

"No, it's not just about a dream. It's about a woman that is going to be murdered."

"What do you want us to do, Pamela? Go over to his home with our guns blazing and arrest him? Are we supposed to issue a search warrant for his home because of your dreams?"

"I'm just asking you to investigate the situation. Just look into it a little bit," said Pam.

"Well, let me ask you this. Has Doctor Percival ever done anything to hurt you?"
"Well, um...no."

"Do you have any physical evidence that Doctor Percival committed any of these crimes?"

"No, I don't have any evidence, but you have to believe me."

"Look Pamela, I know you've been through a lot with your accident and your husband's arrest, but we can't just start arresting citizens when people have bad feelings about them. Doctor Percival has been one of our most distinguished citizens in our community. To accuse somebody like that of committing a crime as serious as murder, you better have some concrete evidence."

"Oh, now I see," said Pam. "It's alright to charge my husband with a crime he didn't commit just because someone said he did it, but not Doctor Percival. My husband works harder than Preston ever had, but you don't consider him a distinguished citizen? Now you have the nerve to talk to me about having evidence. When you find another dead woman in this city, you'll have your evidence."

The lieutenant became annoyed by Pam's comments.

"You just worry about your own household, and let me worry about my district. When you get some evidence, then come and talk to me."

"You don't seem to get it. I'm not asking for a cavalry, lieutenant. All I'm asking is for you to check him out before another person dies."

"I'll see what I can do," said Lieutenant Douglas. "I can't promise you I'll be able to put any manpower into this, but we'll see."

After Pamela left hung up the telephone, the lieutenant remained seated in his chair. He tapped the side of his head with a yellow pencil. 'Something just doesn't add up,' he mumbled. He pulled his jacket off the back of his vinyl chair and rushed out the door. Jumping into his black vehicle, he headed back to the scene where Donald was murdered. Tattered yellow police tape still hung from the trees. The orange outline from Duncan's shells remained, though the evidence had been taken away. Douglas slowly searched through the dirt, pointing out specific areas with the tip of his pencil. He began drawing a diagram. He first mapped the place where the victim was found. From that spot, Douglas followed the footsteps back to the area signifying Duncan's position.

By measuring the depth of the footprint in relation to the other prints, Douglas could see the place Duncan stood for a large amount of time. He noticed a streaking print moving toward Donald. The impression caused by Donald's body proved it was impossibly for Duncan to shoot him. The shot would have to fly over a hill and curve slightly to the left to strike Donald. Douglas knew that was extremely unlikely. He also knew there was no reason for Duncan to run toward his friend if he assassinated him.

He smacked himself in the head, knowing he had jumped to an unforgettable conclusion. The lieutenant scouted the crime scene. He headed to a rarely traveled road a few yards away from the area. Crouching to check the road out, there were only one set of tire tracks within the soil. Lieutenant Douglas walked up and down the road, until he came upon a piece of evidence. The shell from a shotgun lay behind the tracks. He retrieved the shell with the edge of his coat wrapped around his hand. The path from that point was a clear shot to Donald. After placing the shell in his car, the lieutenant took pictures of the area from all angles. There was a strong possibility that an innocent man was in jail, while a killer was free to strike again. Lieutenant Douglas knew he had to make it right. Utilizing a few connections within the police force, the lieutenant was able to get bond posted for Duncan while he organized the evidence to prove him innocent.

Chapter 10

Pam determined that the only way she would be able to retrieve the evidence necessary to force the police into action was to get it herself. She remembered the spare keys Preston gave her to enter his home. If there was a time to use them, she figured this was the time. Pam immediately drove to Preston's home.

His residence was a brick colonial home with four large square windows enforcing the grounds. A smaller window was positioned just beneath the low pitched gable roof. Two white wooden columns surrounded each side of the Brazilian mahogany wood door. A row of hedges lined the perimeter, while the two light posts buried in the soil glowed in the night's sky. The neatness of the property gave a welcoming impression, yet the environment signaled confinement and imprisonment. There was a long curved driveway that rested beside Preston's home.

Slowly, Pam moved through the pathway between the hedges. Preston's car was no where in sight. Her hands trembled as she put the first key into the lock. The key didn't fit the lock. As the second key was inserted, the door was opened. At first glance, Pam could see the home was meticulously kept. Designer sandstone tiles adorned the floor. Pam's footsteps seemed to create more noise than she expected. Moving through the colonial, Pam searched for articles to provide the police concerning Preston's killings. Her search led her to Preston's bedroom. The room contained plush blue carpet, a cherry wood dresser and cabinet set, and two nightstands. In the center was a king size bed covered with blue velvet sheets. The bed looked as if no one had ever slept in it.

Pam explored all of the hiding places, from the top shelves of the closet, to the area between the mattress and the box spring. There was nothing to be found. Before giving up on her search, she decided to look in a more obvious location. Opening each drawer of the large dresser, she found all of Preston's folded socks, his pressed underwear and his neatly ordered ties. After closing the dresser drawers, Pam looked in the cabinet. The top drawer was empty. Crouching to search the bottom drawer, Pam found what she had been looking for.

Yellowing sheets of paper filled the drawer. Each was organized according to the date that was listed along the top edge of the paper. Rambling through them, Pam read a couple of the short notes. The first was a letter written by Jenna to Preston.

"Hey Preston, I just wanted to tell you how sweet you are. Don't worry about those girls picking on you. I think you're great. Someday they'll see how good a guy you are. I'm so glad to hear about your feelings for me. I like you too. If you really want to go out, just give me a call. Jenna."

Her phone number was scribbled just below her name. Pam read another letter from Jenna to Preston.

"Hello Preston, Is everything alright with you? You've been acting really strange since we went out. If there's something on your mind, you can tell me. If I'm supposed to be your friend, let me be there for you. If you don't want to call me, just write me and let me know what's on your mind. Take care, Jenna."

She read the next one.

"Preston, I don't know why you're telling everybody in school we're together. Maybe there would have been a chance, but you have too many issues for me. I think you should take some time to get to know yourself before you seek a relationship. We can still be friends, but I don't think we should pursue anything more than that. Can we still be friends? Jenna."

Looking at another note, the mood of the author seemed to change. It was sent by Jenna to Preston.

"Preston, you have to stop calling me. I know it's you, whether you want to admit it or not. If you want to be some kind of playboy or something, don't call me anymore. I heard about your situation with the girls in school. I think you're letting your ego get the best of you. I thought I knew you, but I guess I don't. No matter what you say, or what you send me, I'm not going out with you. I don't know what's wrong with you, but I can't deal with it. I tried to be your friend, but you're creeping me out. I really don't think we should talk anymore. Jenna."

Looking further into the box, Pamela found several unopened letters from Preston to Jenna. Each one was stamped as returned mail. Pam opened the one on top.

"Dear Jenna,

I called you all day, and your phone was disconnected. I don't know how we're supposed to be in a relationship if you don't call me. I heard you were talking to Rick today. I hope he wasn't asking you out. I would hate to see him have a broken arm or something the day before Homecoming. Anyway, I just wanted to let you know that I'll be free this weekend. I have a lot of things planned for us. Just call me as soon as you can.
Love, Preston."

Pam saw the next letter was sent to Jenna at another address, but was again returned to Preston.

"Dear Jenna,

You can't get away from me. Did you think I wouldn't find your address? I'm very upset with you. First you change your hair color, when you know I don't like blondes. Then you move without letting me know. We're going to have to talk about this. It's driving me crazy, being in a relationship with someone who doesn't show me respect. I'm sure you'll change your mind when I finish medical school. One day we'll have the house with the white picket fence and everything. I know that's what you want, and I want it too. You can't keep living like you're single. You're with me now. This better be the last time you make any changes in your life without my permission. If you don't write me back, I'm going to be very upset. I don't think you want to see me when I'm angry. Love, Preston."

Pam found a picture that was set in a wooded area. Dense trees surrounded a river and large rocks were embedded within the soil. Near the center of the photo, a woman's body could be seen through the fog. The body had begun to sink, but the photographer took time to capture the moment. Flipping to the next picture, she viewed a photograph shot closer to the woman. Her blonde hair was matted and wet, and her blue shirt had blood stains throughout its fibers. She was lying on her back near a cloudy body of water. From the expressionless look on her face, as well as her pale features, Pam could see that her life had been expired for some time. The features of the woman became more prevalent as she continued to scrutinize the photo. Through her mind, Pam reconciled the body was that of the woman named Jenna. Pam held the picture next to her face, comparing her face to Jenna's photo. Even though the vibrancy of life was in contrast to the death displayed in the picture, the connection was unmistakable.

As she attempted to decipher the evidence, Pam heard the sound of a vehicle's engine entering the driveway. Rushing to the small window in the center of the building, Pam saw a black SUV parking. Pam grabbed the doctor's telephone, and called Lieutenant Douglas. The lieutenant was driving with his partner in the front seat, and Duncan in the back seat. The officers were giving Duncan a ride home from the precinct, when the lieutenant's personal cell phone rang.

"This is Douglas," said the lieutenant.

"Lieutenant Douglas, this is Pam. I need your help."

"I'm helping you as we speak, Pam. I took care of the situation, so you won't have to worry about it."

When Duncan heard the lieutenant mention Pam's name, he inched up toward the front seat. His attempt to listen irritated Officer Davis, who pounded the plastic divider in the car.

"That's not it, just listen," Pam screamed. She saw the doctor moving toward the front door, and hung up the telephone to look for a hiding place.

"Hello, Pam," said the lieutenant. "Pam, are you there?"
There was no answer. Only the dial tone was heard from the other end.

"What's wrong with Pam?" asked Duncan.

"I don't know, but you guys can talk about it when we drop you off.
The trio soon arrived at Duncan's house, and the lieutenant let him out of the back seat of the police vehicle.

"Just stay out of trouble. We have a lot of work to do to keep you out of jail."
He patted Duncan on the shoulder, before driving off.

Duncan walked in his home, looking around the house.

"Pam, are you here? Pam, where are you?"
Walking over to the kitchen counter, he saw some of Pam's medical papers. Dr. Percival's name was printed on the top of the page, with a circled address listed just beneath it. The address was 3131 West Treeland Road. Duncan looked outside,

observing his truck with flat tires and deep gouges in the paint. He jumped in the truck, and drove it toward the doctor's address. The vehicle flopped sluggishly down the road, with the tread clinging to the rim.

Pam turned to grab all of the papers within the drawer, but there were too many to contain. She tugged at the handle, until the whole drawer came loose. Holding the drawer in her left hand, Pamela sprinted down the stairs, clinging to Preston's belongings.

Throughout her haste, letters fluttered through the air, littering the carpet. As she met the door, a key was heard being inserted into the lock. Pam froze, fear restraining her from her escape. The knob of the brass lined door was turned, and it was pushed open from the outside. Through the entrance walked Preston, his eyes slowly rotating and locking on Pam. The corner of his mouth twisted upward to form a demented smile.

Sensibility hit Pam. She darted into the next room, dropping more of Preston's mementos along the hallway.

Pam, you don't have to run. I would never hurt you," said Preston, extracting his scalpel from the pocket of his trench coat. One by one, he obsessively retrieved each item dropped by Pam. Preston neatly place one on top of the other. He turned the lock on the front door behind him, preventing Pam's exit. Patiently, Preston followed her, while Pam tried each and every potential exit within his home.

Preston had large brass locks fixed to each of the windows. Any entrance or exit by Pam would have taken the key held within his possession. The evidence of the lock's strength was given by Pam's inability to open them, despite trying with all her strength. Running toward the door leading to the rear exit, Pam was dismayed to find a maddening number of locks. She ran back up the steps, slamming the door in the face of Preston. The doctor kicked the door back into Pam, who fell back into the wall of Preston's bedroom.

Within the terror displayed on Pam's face, the similarities between Pamela and Jenna seemed to be magnified. Preston recalled that Jenna had the same expression in her last moments.

"It's alright Jenna," said the delusional doctor.

"I told you I wouldn't hurt you. Not unless you make me."

He extended his hand to Pam, with a sincere expression on his face. She was fixed to the wall, looking around the room for an escape.

"How could you do this?" Pam asked.

"You're supposed to save lives, not take lives."

There was a faint knock on the door. Preston put his finger near his lips, urging Pam to remain quiet. He locked his hand around her wrist.

"If you make a sound, I promise I'll kill you."

"I won't say anything," Pam whispered.

As Preston loosened his grip, Pam slapped his hand away and began to scream.

"Help me. Somebody help me," said Pam, climbing across the bed.

She picked up some of Preston's letters, holding them with both hands. Preston stepped toward Pam, but moved away as she clutched the papers.

"Are you afraid I'm going to rip them or something?" asked Pam.
She held the papers as if they were a hostage in a bank heist.

"Alright, I'm setting it down," said Preston. He slowly placed the scalpel on the floor. Kicking it away from the area, the doctor raised his hands.
Just give me my letters, and I'll let you go."

It was then that Pam heard the sound of a loud boom near the front door. She hoped it was a horde of police coming to her rescue. Over and over again, the noise was heard. Preston shielded her from exiting the room. An explosive burst came from downstairs, shaking the foundation of the structure. Pamela dashed around the side of the bed, nearly passing Preston. He reached out, grasping a handful of her dark blue jacket.

While Pam attempted to pull away from the doctor, Preston refused to let go. She turned to face Preston, forcibly swinging her leg toward his groin. Doctor Percival sidestepped her advance and pulled her by her arm. She caught hold of Preston's finger, twisting it in an awkward direction. Pam's aggressiveness caught him off guard. Her fear provided a rush of adrenaline that snapped the bone of Preston's finger. He yelped in pain, biting his lip and momentarily releasing Pam from her confinement.

She ran toward the stairs and the sound of heavy footsteps on the floor just below. As she reached the stairs, Pam saw Duncan near the bottom of the banister. She quickly moved on to the first step, until Preston grabbed her by her collar.

"Pam," screamed Duncan.

His wife held on to the banister, attempting to maintain her balance. Preston looked down the stairs, appalled by the site of Duncan.

"So this is what you left me for, Jenna? A fat ass guy like that? Tell him that I'm the one you're with now. Tell him it's over between the two of you. Tell him you love me."

He pulled the collar of Pam's windbreaker so tight, it caused her to choke.

"I don't love you," Pam whispered.

Preston's face began to twitch. He increased the strain on Pam's throat.

"You do love me, don't you Jenna?"

Duncan hesitated to move forward, aware that Preston had Pam on the edge of falling.

"Let go of me," Pam whispered. "And my name's not Jenna."

Every anger filled emotion Preston felt with Jenna was reincarnated through Pam. He dropped his head, shaking it from side to side. His grip on am diminished, and she could feel the air surge into her lungs. As Pam took a step toward Duncan, Preston reestablished his hold.

"So you don't love me?" Preston asked.

She lunged toward the next steps, when Preston reared back and pushed her down. As she tumbled down the stairs, Pam reached up to grab the banister. Duncan rushed forward to break Pam's fall, but only after her head had smacked against two of the steps. She rested in Duncan's arms, dazed but still conscious. A large cut was opened just above her left eye, and a stream of blood ran down the side of her face.

"Pam, are you alright?" asked Duncan.

"Pam, look at me."

He turned his head to face him, but it dropped to the side. Preston smiled at Duncan.

"If I can't have her, do you really think I'm gonna let you have her?"

Duncan gently laid Pam against the living room wall. He took a long look at his wife, and turned toward Preston. Doctor Percival patiently walked down the steps while removing his trench coat. Turning to see his front door in shambles, Preston grinned at Duncan.

"So you did that to my door? That's pretty impressive. I'd like to see if you could do that to me."

He rolled the sleeves of his white dress shirt up to his forearms. Five feet away from each other, the two men visually sparred. They faced each other, moving in a large semicircle. Duncan moved first, reaching for the sleeve of Preston's shirt. Preston ducked under his arms, thrusting his elbow into Duncan's ribs. The impact of the blow instantly broke two ribs. Duncan held his arm near his left side. He coughed, as he attempted to gather his breath.

He lunged toward the doctor with his outstretched right arm. Preston danced to the side, playfully mocking Duncan. He slapped Duncan on the side of his face, leaving a large read mark for added humiliation. Preston bounced on the tips of his toes, swaying back and forth. Every instance Duncan surged toward the doctor, Preston would slap him.

When the entertainment value of the doctor's defensive moves wore thin, Preston began to strike Duncan harder. A ridge hand to the face, followed by a punch to the jaw, and later several kicks to the back of the head formed the violent ensemble. Bruised and beaten, Duncan had no success catching the quick and more athletic Doctor Percival. His martial arts proved to be more than Duncan could physically handle.

Panting against the wall of Preston's great room, the wheels within Duncan's mind began to turn.

"I don't know if I'll make it through this alive," said Duncan.

"Don't worry about that. I'm going to let you live for a while. Why should I rush through this? I plan on breaking each and every bone in your body before I kill you, so just be patient."

Duncan pulled himself off the wall.

"You know what the sad thing is? No matter what you do, Pam still won't love you. She'll still love me."

Preston's expression changed. His eyes bulged at Duncan, and he clenched his fists.

"Even if I'm dead, she'll still mourn me," said Duncan. "You can't make her love you."

With her head still clouded, Pam crawled to the telephone in the kitchen. She once again called the direct line of Lieutenant Douglas. "Hello, this is Douglas."

"3131 West Treeland Road," said Pam.

"Excuse me, what did you say."

"It's Pam. 3131 West Treeland Road."

She collapsed to the floor, with the telephone crashing and breaking in pieces.

"I've had enough of this," said Preston.

He was rattled, and ran toward his large combatant. Duncan remained stationary with his hands to his side, as Preston approached.

When Preston was a foot away, Duncan exploded into him with his right shoulder. Preston flew onto the floor, remaining there for a few moments. For more than fifteen minutes, they wrestled on the floor. Preston finally sprang to his feet and rushed Duncan. Duncan was finally able to grab hold of him, bear hugging him as tightly as possible, until a sharp kick from Preston struck Duncan's ribs. He dropped Preston on to the floor. With his knee pressed into Preston's chest, Duncan continued to strike him in the face. Preston squirmed and dodged as many blows as he could, but Duncan's weight allowed him to connect a number of times. His thoughts concerning the man who nearly ended Pam's life enraged him.

"Fontain," someone shouted from behind Duncan. He turned around to see Lieutenant Douglas and Officer Davis standing just within the front door. Officer Davis pointed his firearm at Duncan.

"Step away from him, Fontain," he screamed.

Duncan slowly raised his hands. Hearing a whimper within the next room, the lieutenant slowly walked away from his companion and toward the kitchen. He turned to Officer Davis, signaling his intention to check out the kitchen.

"Go ahead, I got this under control," said the officer.

Lieutenant Douglas had his weapon drawn, as he held it with his arms slightly bent and his head tilted. He dipped around the angles of each corner, following the smeared streak of blood stretching from the great room to the kitchen. Visually securing the room, Lieutenant Douglas found Pam on the cold laminate floor. Blood continued to drip from the wound on her forehead.

The cordless telephone was broken, and pieces surrounded her body. With his eyes focused horizontally, he crouched near Pam. Placing his fingers on the left side of her neck, the lieutenant checked Pam's pulse. He moved them just below her nostrils, where he could feel the slight breath of life.

"Mrs. Fontain, can you hear me?" asked the lieutenant. "Pam, say something."

Pam was flat on the ground. The side of her face rested against the floor. She opened her eyes, struggling to look at the lieutenant.

"Who did this to you, Pam?" he asked.

Pam softly moaned.

"Pamela, you have to tell me who did this to you."

"Preston," Pam whispered.

In the great room, Duncan followed the officer's commands to move away from Preston after giving him one more punch to the jaw.

"Put your hands on the back of your head and step away from the doctor," said Officer Davis.

"But officer, I'm not..."

"Shut up, Fontain. I don't have this gun pointed at your head for cheap thrills. I have no problems shooting you."

Duncan held his hands over his head, locking them behind his neck. Preston spit the blood out of his mouth and smiled, as Duncan moved toward the wall. Officer Davis trailed Duncan, forcing him against the far wall. Their backs were turned away from Preston, while

Davis nonchalantly frisked Duncan with his let hand.

Searching the room, Preston saw the vintage scalpel underneath the wooden trim of the near wall a few feet away. He scurried over to it, hiding it against his hand and wrist. Hearing a rustling from behind the officer, Duncan twisted his head to find its source. From the corner of his eye, he could see Preston rising to his feet. He turned toward Preston, but the distracted officer pushed Duncan back against the wall. While Preston crept from behind, the officer reached for his handcuffs. Each time Duncan attempted to mention the doctor's approach, Officer Davis pushed his face into the wall.

Preston stood two feet away, brandishing the razor sharp scalpel. Duncan reacted, swiping the cuffs away from Officer Davis. He turned to confront Doctor Percival. The officer's gun nearly fell from his grasp. Duncan turned to grab the weapon, but the officer moved it out of his reach. Briefly fumbling with the firearm, Officer Davis twice pulled the trigger. The sound of the blasts echoed through the house. Holding his large wound, Duncan fell to his knees. The sound of gunfire brought Lieutenant Douglas out of the kitchen.

Duncan fell inches away from the officer, who continued to point his gun at the wounded man.

"Lay face down on the ground," he yelled.

From behind the officer, Preston exposed the scalpel. He drew back his arm, stabbing Officer Davis in the shoulder blade. The officer shrieked in pain, reaching for the wound. The gun fell to the floor. Arching his back, Officer Davis twirled around. Preston swung the scalpel upward, driving it into the officer's chest. Seeing his partner bleeding from the front and back, Lieutenant Douglas aimed his gun at the would-be killer.

As Preston reached back for another attack, the lieutenant fired his Glock. The bullet entered his shoulder, exiting through the other side and embedding itself in the wall. Preston continued to wildly swipe at the officer, grazing him with each swing.

Lieutenant Douglas pulled the trigger again, releasing two more rounds. Both bullets lodged inside Preston's body. He stared at the spots the bullets entered with a confused expression that spoke to his shock through the situation.

"Put down the knife," Douglas shouted.

The blood began to pour from Preston's wounds. He fell to one knee, slowly bowing his head. Still clutching the scalpel, he looked toward the lieutenant. Through his red stained teeth, the doctor shouted.

"Shoot me, dammit go ahead and shoot me. You don't have control over me. I determine who lives and who dies, not you. I'm ready to die right now."

Preston dropped to both knees, spitting out a gob of blood. While he tried to gather himself for one more attack, Lieutenant Douglas prepared to fire a fatal shot. The blood loss took its toll on Doctor Percival. His eyes rolled in the back of his head and he collapsed, his body twitching along the floor. Lieutenant Douglas scanned the area. The three men lay on the floor, each one on the verge of death. Within his blood soiled home, only the lieutenant remained standing. He pulled his radio from his belt.

"Officer down, dispatch. Lieutenant Douglass to dispatch, officer down. I need immediate backup and some paramedics."

On the other end, the dispatcher confirmed his request.

"Don't worry, Lieutenant. Help is on the way," said the dispatcher.

Chapter 11

It had been a few months since the incident, and painful wounds gave way to a renewed vitality. Both Pamela and Duncan were relieved to have their troubles behind them. Preston was removed from their lives, and every charge against Duncan was dismissed. They drove down the highway, accompanied by the blue skies above them. The couple embraced the anticipation of their first vacation in ten years, celebrating the Fourth of July holiday. They looked forward to renewing their vows upon their return. Duncan lovingly held Pam's hand, while she rested her head against his shoulder.

In his lap, she held a sketchbook with pages of unfinished sketches. Physically unable to sculpt, this form of art had been her release while she recovered from her injuries. The constant rumbling of the engine enhanced the urge to sleep for Pam. She assumed a rest filled ride would be given to her. As she began to nod off, Pam looked down at her sketches. The various lines on the paper began to take form, until a picture came together. When Pamela looked down at the sketchbook, she saw the face of a bearded man staring at her. She was speechless.

"What's wrong?" asked Duncan.

With a blank expression on her face, she turned to her husband.

Pressing the button to let down her automatic window, Pam began to crumble her papers. She tossed each out of the window, watching them fly through the air. The papers hit the ground and were run over by the semi-truck following behind them. The driver blew his horn, angered by the airborne debris.

"Honey, what's wrong?"

Pam looked at Duncan, patting him on his knee.

"Nothing Duncan," she answered. "Absolutely nothing. Just keep driving."

She rested her head on the shoulder of her husband, as the continued driving down the blacktop highway.

The stagnant smell within the four walls consistently reinforced his reality. Freedom was a vague memory, more difficult to recall with each passing day. There would be forty more years without a chance for parole to put the scattered pieces of his mind back together. It was his punishment for killing Officer Davis and attempting to kill Pamela. For a man that had grown so private, the packs of caged men mere feet away from each other drew the life from him every day. Suffocation in the claustrophobic environment persisted.

There were no thoughts of an alternate path derived from contrasting choices. Every reflection surrounded payback. There was a need for payback against Duncan, against the police, and every person who put him in this forsaken place of residence. It all began with Pamela. Not a day passed without him carving a mark in his makeshift calendar. When the guards took away his writing utensil, a broken tooth brush, and his own blood became his ink. No longer a clean shaven doctor, Preston's scraggly beard gave him the appearance of a wild man. His intense blue eyes darted in every direction. Becoming increasingly erratic, the inmate began causing commotions. He screamed throughout each night for the two weeks without ceasing. The guard's reaction was to beat him into submission. From nightsticks to laundry bags filled with rocks, the prison guards found creative ways to encourage his silence. Even the harsh discipline from the guards failed to disrupt the noise.

By the time he was taken for evaluation, he had killed an inmate and seriously injured two guards. Though the doctor's were unable to find psychological evidence of Preston's insanity, his episodes of violence gave reason to institutionalize him. Preston was taken out of the prison and placed in a psychiatric ward. When the next inmate took over Preston's former cell, his eyes caught hold of the bloody messages written within the etched calendar. It was behind the lower bunk bed. He moved the mattress out of the way to see the rest of the calendar. On the block for May 3rd, the name "Tank" was written. Tank was Preston's roommate, and one of the toughest inmates in the prison. His body was found inside a duct in the prison's boiler room. Listed in the June 10th section was the names "Gino" and "Bailey". These were the two guards responsible for covering Preston's wing of the prison, and the main men responsible for his discipline. The warden discovered both men were beaten with a mop handle and left in the laundry room. He looked closer at the calendar. There was a note written on the July 4th column. In that slot was the blood smeared name, Pam.

QUICK ORDER FORM

Limbus list price $12.95

Website: www.vaughanworks.com

Email orders- vaughanworks1@mfire.com

Telephone Orders- Call 1-877-VAWORKS (829-6757) toll free.

Postal Orders- VAUGHANWORKS, Julian Hampton, PO Box 18511-0511, Milwaukee, WI 53218, USA

Shipping by air-

U.S.: Please add $3.00 for the first book and $2.00 for each additional product.
International: Please add $6.00 for the first book, and $4.00 for each additional book (estimate).

For speaking engagements, seminars, interviews, or any of the Vaughanworks services, call, email, or mail request to the addresses listed above.

.